D1593445

The Poetry Collection

A gift from
Mr. Desmond McLean

Keith and Shirley Campbell Library

Rowan
University

ROUTINE DISRUPTIONS

also by Kenward Elmslie

Bare Bones, Bamberger Books, 1995

Postcards on Parade, Bamberger Books, 1993

Pay Dirt, with Joe Brainard, Bamberger Books, 1992

Sung Sex, with Joe Brainard, Kulchur Foundation, 1990

26 Bars, with Donna Dennis, Z Press, 1987

Three Sisters, a libretto, Z Press, 1987

Bimbo Dirt, with Ken Tisa, Z Press, 1982

Moving Right Along, Z Press, 1980

Communications Equipment, Burning Deck, 1979

The Alphabet Work, Titanic Books, 1977

Topiary Trek, with Karl Torok, Topia Press, 1977

Washington Square, a libretto, Belwin-Mills, 1976

Tropicalism, Z Press, 1975

The Seagull, a libretto, Belwin-Mills, 1974

The Sweet Bye and Bye, a libretto, Boosey & Hawkes, 1973

The Orchid Stories, Doubleday & Co., 1973 / Z Press, 1975

The Grass Harp, a musical play, Samuel French, 1972

Shiny Ride, with Joe Brainard, Boke Press, 1972

City Junket, a play, Adventures in Poetry, 1972 / Bamberger Books, 1987

Motor Disturbance, Columbia University Press, 1971 / Full Court Press, 1978

Circus Nerves, Black Sparrow Press, 1971

Girl Machine, Angel Hair, 1971

Album, with Joe Brainard, Kulchur Press, 1969

The Champ, with Joe Brainard, Black Sparrow Press, 1968 / The Figures, 1994

Power Plant Poems, with Joe Brainard, C Press, 1967

The 1967 Gamebook Calendar, with Joe Brainard, Boke Press, 1967

Miss Julie, a libretto, Boosey & Hawkes, 1965

Lizzie Borden, a libretto, Boosey & Hawkes, 1965

The Baby Book, with Joe Brainard, Boke Press, 1965

Pavilions, Tibor de Nagy Editions, 1961

KENWARD ELMSLIE

Routine Disruptions
selected poems & lyrics 1960-1998

Edited by W.C. BAMBERGER

 COFFEE HOUSE PRESS : : MINNEAPOLIS

The front cover collage is adapted from *Act One Curtain, #9* in Kenward Elmslie's *Postcards on Parade* series.

The poems and lyrics collected here appeared in the following books: *Circus Nerves, Album, Motor Disturbance, Tropicalism, Moving Right Along,* and *Sung Sex.*

Music credits for song lyrics and libretto excerpts, and credits for poet-artist collaborations appear on pages 255–256 along with publication acknowledgments for previously uncollected poems.

Coffee House Press is supported in part by a grant provided by the Minnesota State Arts Board, through an appropriation by the Minnesota State Legislature, and in part by a grant from the National Endowment for the Arts. Significant support has also been provided by the McKnight Foundation; Lannan Foundation; Jerome Foundation; Target Stores, Dayton's, and Mervyn's by the Dayton Hudson Foundation; General Mills Foundation; The St. Paul Companies; Butler Family Foundation; Honeywell Foundation; Star Tribune Foundation; James R. Thorpe Foundation; Dain Bosworth Foundation; Pentair, Inc.; Beverly J. and John A. Rollwagen Fund of the Minneapolis Foundation; the Peter & Madeleine Martin Foundation; the law firm of Schwegman, Lundberg, Woessner & Kluth, P.A.; and many individual donors. To you and our many readers across the country, we send our thanks for your continuing support.

Coffee House Press books are available to the trade through our primary distributor, Consortium Book Sales & Distribution, 1045 Westgate Drive, Saint Paul, MN 55114. For personal orders, catalogs, or other information, write to Coffee House Press, 27 N. 4th Street, Suite 400, Minneapolis, MN 55401.

LIBRARY OF CONGRESS CIP DATA
Elmslie, Kenward.
    Routine disruptions : selected poems & lyrics 1960-1998 / Kenward Elmslie;   edited by W.C. Bamberger.
        p.   cm.
    ISBN 1-56689-077-2 (alk. paper)
    I. Bamberger, W.C. II. Title.
    PS3509.L715R68   1998   98-21157
811'.54—dc21   CIP
10 9 8 7 6 5 4 3 2 1

printed in Canada

Contents

i-iii **Trek Aids: An Introduction**

from **Circus Nerves**

17   Circus Nerves & Worries

18   Communique for Orpheus

22   City of My Dinge World, Venice

24   Ancestor Worship

26   Fringe People

27   Halloween Loop

28   Nov 25

30   Awake on March 27th

32   First Frost

from **Album**

35   White Attic

36   Four Scenarios

38   Aztec Dinner Dance

40   Revolutionary Letter

42   Breech Baby

44   Paper Suns

Poem Songs

47   Air

48   Bio

50   Eggs

52   Sin in the Hinterlands

54   Bang-Bang Tango

56   Sneaky Pete

58   And I Was There

59   Adele The Vaudeville Martinet

60   Meat

61   Girl Machine

from **Motor Disturbance**

69 Fruit

70 The Dustbowl

72 History of France

76 Shirley Temple Surrounded by Lions

78 The Power Plant Sestina

80 Japanese City

82 Jan 24

84 Feathered Dancers

86 Fig Mill

90 Motor Disturbance

from **Tropicalism**

95 Routine Disruption

96 Middle Class Fantasies

98 Winter Life

104 Visual Radios

106 Time Lags

108 Coda

109 Tropicalism

Song Lyrics I

121 Lie With Me, Sweet John

122 They

124 Brazil

126 One Night Stand

128 Marry With Me

130 Who'll Prop Me Up in the Rain

132 Andrei's Lament

134 Beauty Secrets

from **Moving Right Along**

137 Easter Poem for Joe '79

138 Squatter in the Foreground

139 Black Froth

142 Monster Worship I

143 Monster Worship II

144 Communications Equipment

146 August

148 In The Sky

150 One Hundred I Remembers

from **Sung Sex**

159 Four Vermont Haikus

160 Nov 17

161 Pullmanette

162 Rug Boast

164 Kitchen

166 Mindless Bliss

169 The Thirties

170 The Sixties

Song Lyrics II

177 Schlock 'n' Sleaze R&B

181 Seventeen Years of Living Hell

186 Moments in Time

188 Take Me Away, Roy Rogers

191 It's A Good Life

194 Lads

198 Somdomite

202 A Secret Sacred Niche

204 Love Song

Poems 1991—1998

207   Champ Dust

220   Bare Bones

230   Animals in the Walls

231   Spring in Argentina

232   Local Branch

234   Jakarta Night Arrival

236   Sunday in Dunedin

239   Welcome Home

240   Rummage Sale

241   Panopticon for Calamity Winifred

242   Outback Taunt

246   Forty Sonnet

247   Fiscal Nonsense

252   Happy Re-Return

Trek Aids: An Introduction

Your trek through this selection of the poetry and lyrics of
Kenward Elmslie will not be the same as mine, nor will my
next be the same one I took in gathering together this assem-
bly of varied terrains—a multivoiced poetry turf that includes
visually shaped poems, "Girl Machine," pure language, "Rug
Boast," found poems, "Fig Mill," culled from a pulp magazine
for rural housewives, joke-rhyme doggerel, "Bio," travel poems,
"Tropicalism"—The Amazon, and love poems, "Bare Bones"
—about his life with and the death of Joe Brainard. The works
range from an extremely demanding, wilderness-dense prose
poem, "Champ Dust" to easy-to-read snapshots, "Four Ver-
mont Haikus," plain factual autobiography, "One Hundred I
Remembers" vs. the bulk of his poetry, where facts and real-life
time are layered in, often obliquely, so there is the ferment of
constant interplay between the recording of mind's eye visions
and the reportage of outer actualities.

Elmslie's first career was that of musical theater wordsmith. Get
used to slang and coinages, to neologisms and archaisms and
importations, to shop talk and the lingo of inside information,
because they're the anything-but-fossil fuel on which many of
these poems and song lyrics run. Friendships struck up with
poets Kenneth Koch, James Schuyler, Barbara Guest, Frank
O'Hara, and John Ashbery led Elmslie into writing poetry in
the interregnums when he had no show-writing chores. By the
time the first poem collected here was published, Elmslie had
written the librettos for two produced operas, *The Sweet Bye and
Bye* and *Lizzie Borden*. By the time of *Album*, his first full-length
collection, a third opera, *Miss Julie*, had been produced. *The
Grass Harp*, a musical play, based on the novel by Truman
Capote, for which he'd written the book and lyrics, was headed
for Broadway, and *Lovewise*, one of his lyrics, had been a juke-
box hit for Nat King Cole. Elmslie has continued to write in

these (and other) forms for more than three decades now. At times, he has combined the two worlds, and set his poetry to music—several tapes and albums of his poems and lyrics have been issued, with music by Elmslie and by the composers he's written words for. The lyrics illuminate something vital to his work in all its forms: the stance of musical theater as loyal opposition, both celebrating and mocking the ways of our culture. In his poetry, these opposites attract, clash like flint and steel, and poetry is the spark that flies—

> Up to us
> To link up disparate inner workings of you and me.
> Accentuate if-you-can-step-in-it-you-can-eat-it dialectic.
> Eliminate let-me-sew-you-to-your-sheet syndrome.
> —*from* "In The Sky"

Sober and mocking. In his poetry, as in his life, emotions rarely stand alone. He likes to pair them off, trio them off, quartet—whether they appear simultaneously, as above, or back-to-back—

> just as this morning we awoke in a spoon position
> you and I
>
> unfolded unthinkingly and dispersed
> for another time's-up type day
> —*from* "Jan 24"

the conflicting emotions and shifting tones of his poems capture the routine disruptions we all live through and by. And while doing so, these poems remain playful. Which is not to say they are always fun.

John Ashbery once wrote Elmslie's poetry is like the notes of "a mad scientist who has swallowed the wrong potion in his lab and is desperately trying to get his calculations on paper before everything closes in." This perfectly captures the tone of, for instance, "Champ Dust"—

> Expert consensus—whirligig snippets are whooping it up
> down in the tracts. Constant prowl for more fodder. If host

killed, they kaput. It's that simple. Not easy find new
palazzo, groaning sideboard well stocked with devourables—
forget candelabras. Baked Alaska munchies served at room
temp. Humpy footmen forbidden groin contact or "Have
A Nice Day" solecisms, and (does anyone still read Emily
Post?) after the ladies have repaired to the pergola, no
soft porn reruns of MM funeral home Last Rites. Golly
Grrr. This is so New Age—demotic muddle headlong,
normal functions scrambled . . .

The subject is an episode of illness. What is unmistakably
Elmslie here—in addition to the torque-by-compression of
"Constant prowl," "Not easy find" etc.—is how even the most
serious of subjects is given spin through language play:
"kaput," "Golly Grrr." This may at first read seem like self-
consciousness, but there is a bigger answer to the "why" of this
mad scientist lingo: survival. Because play is about survival as
much as is the more well-traveled road of Mad Maxism. In the
poem song "Bio," Elmslie observes that

Trek   aids
Sped up the decades

for him. These works, in addition to the great pleasure to be
gained from their whirling up-and-at-'em language, their
smile-provoking shifts of perspective from the formal to the
slaphappy, will make invaluable trek aids in the coming, even
more sped-up decades. Kenward Elmslie's poems and song
lyrics await you, purring with potential energy, rarin' to go, to
accompany and console, cheer and guide you anywhere you
might go, at your service for decades to come.

— W.C. Bamberger

from

Circus Nerves

Circus Nerves & Worries

When that everybody's legal twin Mrs. Trio
enters the casino, I expect personal disaster.
Out of next winter's worst blizzard I'm convinced
into the lobby and up the ladder she'll hustle
holding that squeaky velvet purse to one ear.
Placing one green and black peppermint-striped chip
gingerly on zero, zero it is. Which is when I fall dead.
In my shower while soaping. This very next year.

Goony intuition? Well, once in April at the Café Jolie
pointblank she asked: this terror at time in your eyes,
wouldn't crossing a river help? How about now?
Give up my innocence hunt, I exclaimed,
intimacies with failure, all my "sudden magic" hopes?
And today came this dream about moths, I lied,
mouthing, yes wisdoms. Only how to read their lips? Tell me! Tell me!
I dream about vines, she said. Thank you and *ciao*.

Yesterday I looked at my body. Fairly white
Today fairly white, the same. No betterment.
Why can't I feel air? Or take in mountains?
I lose my temper at pine needles, such small stabs.
Breezes scratch me (different from feeling)
and I long to breathe water. Agenda tomorrow:
cable her care of casino TIME TERROR GONE
STOP SEAWEED DREAM GREAT STOP (actually, a lie).

Communique for Orpheus

My Army likes you so much. The young cadets
   in their handsome yellow boots
   and kepis and sashes . . .

My Army how to explain, my very own Army,
   the orderlies, the nurses, the countermen,
   the laundresses, their new silence?

My Army loves you I think. Whether they be pursers,
   mechanics, eye doctors, night watchmen,
   those iron-faced officers . . .

My Army feels sick today. The men are all grumbling,
   they want to join your side—you!—and then
   celebrate victory with fireworks and parades.
   They request a photo of your singing voice
   for the imminent fireworks and parades.
   Candies of you are welcome in case of
   fireworks and parades, as are any movies
   of you yourself chewing smiling etc.
   even sleeping etc. for the about-to-commence
   fireworks and parades.

■

"His whole army is infatuated, infatuated.
A silly god rose out of the sea, made out of
sexy tin with bandages here and there
and it makes hitherto unheard-of sounds,
and changes into man, woman, God, money,
disease, social justice, Beauty—at will!
O where is the country heading,
and what can I, a mere man do?"
                    —George Washington

■

My Army likes you so much. The young cadets
   in their handsome yellow boots
   and kepis and sashes
   call you obscenities softly. Dedicated?
   There is no raillery in the latrines,
   and in their sleep they moan
   madonna madonna.

My Army loves you I think. At strategy conferences,
   those iron-faced officers thrash out
   memories of your tinniest sounds.
   Tears fall on crucial mountains.
   Dilemmas of survival . . .

■

"I hear the sound of mandolins.
Let me fly away with you."
                —Theodore Roosevelt

■

My Army keeps busy.
   Man 20 feet. Man 20 feet. Man 20 feet.
   Guarding pipelines
   from desert area to
   industrial complex.
   Testing sirens, scrubbing sirens, painting sirens,
   guarding the oils and gases necessary
   for the siren system, and so the years
   pass and pass.

My Army likes you so much.
   If state secrets arrive
   in food, lightbulbs, street refuse
   thank the spies
   who vie with each other for blueprints.

Who envy the corridor-like structure
Of your chicaneries.
Who despise all who can hear your voice
in the threshing machines,
the midday boiler explosions,
the violin rallies.

∎

"An enemy trick rose out of the sea,
and his whole army went swimming.
Phooey. Bronze somersaults.
Tonight they returned in silence.
Hellish bivouac, blast the tom-toms.
Meanwhile the animals thump and wheeze,
circling round our tiny encampment,
and the birds with their red beaks
screech and screech, and I wonder
how long can I keep the capitol inviolate?"

—Douglas MacArthur

∎

My Army loves you I think.
But for fun it takes bus expeditions
through the colossal Ice Zoo.
Perfectly preserved, two black pumas
locked in mortal combat. Two penguins
locked in mortal combat. Perfectly preserved
monkeys and birds, long extinct species,
perfectly preserved, each in its own ice segment,
locked in mortal combat, perfectly preserved.
O dirty bus windows, let them see out!

My Army sends you this historic painting
"Painting of You" . . .
BOOM!
My Army likes you so much

loves you I think so much
they are marching to your hit recording ME!
Hurry, when will US be released?
Panic is spreading, what will it sound like?
A bleep, a sobby kid, two whole peoples?
How to know. How to know.
Hurry, is it smashed?
Help! Where is it? Help!
They my army wants to shout
hello into your navel
(Help!) and hear that old song
(Help!) come out to explain
(Help!) the seasons
(Help!) harvests
(Help!) plus certain facts about storms that start
(Help!) (Help!) on the (They can kill!) moon.

City of My Dinge World, Venice

O barbiturates of the north
    let the locals keep their mandalas simple:
    a crystal of bone
    floodlit yet itself
    plus birds waiting, as if aligned for sunset—
    a pastorale devoid of guilt.

Ingrates! Those diagram dots
    forming pulley-shaped pulleys are (ach!) pulleys—
    the Ferris wheel tone of the establishment
    can lead to tremendous illness.
    Ach! You people see only
    Birds Hanging Sideways on Crystal of Bone
    evading the mirror pieces sideways,
    one mirror piece per beak held so, sideways,
    infinite yet serene avenues of further bones and birds,
    whole vistas of trickery,
    and the platforms, the platforms,
    wheeling around to music, bumping often.
    The vertigo inherent in the noise—

    Miss it? With that were-there-air-enough-for-wind totter?
    Miss it? As if the whole were camouflaged as sky?

So. I am scraping off leaf mold, off poor gondola!
    Where, where, where are the houses of pleasure, real pleasure—
    the northern adolescents with their Swiss apertures
    cannot understand the unwholesome yet deft summer encounters:
    pornographic beadwork, so much upkeep,
    mosaics of their initials made public.
    Meanwhile the hunchbacks go uninstitutionalized.

Sweet thieves,
    the pigeons, must they home in those black mouths
    in towers of stone? Their entrance,
    the muffled way they vanish,
    is like the moment of one's death,
    and would chill the normalcy of any noon
    into a mad black scene of crystals falling, all unique.

Ancestor Worship

They advanced towards Point A,
their malicious grandfather. What a purposeful safari: sundry treaties,
water rights, the key to the code to be firmed.

A trail of their old kid gloves
hurled at ferns—any green branch, grrr—did beckon them back.
How often fronds, let go too soon, slashed their cheeks!

Deeper they fled and soon their blond wrist hair
as if from boyish match tricks, frizzled and curled,
charred by the spike-like ping of the jungle wind.

Their gifts were devoured, the weeklies by beetles,
rendering any new stance for Point A impossible. Ants chomped at
the jigsaw puzzles, ground with their hideous mandibles

treey landscapes and Venices at sunset, crunched at
gift vitamin packages, mobile replicas of lares and penates,
gaunt and swinging, all for Point A,

chomped and chomped up their changes of clothes
now three four five sizes too big, why? Why? WHY? Continued next week?
No one could eat or sleep or complete

the act of love, so mostly they discussed
their new diseases, compared hallucinations. The young master
coughed himself inside out one day, and bravo!

rematerialized as a red cactus, with string growths.
The bearers hooted, one by one vanished when new maps brought out
proved Point A was only a waterfall

behind which grandfather sat naked and cooled,
singing of traffic organized like a factory, rashly.
    On heavy afternoons, monkeys brought the group tidbits,

    litters tilted so, forming a shelter against rain,
and the group'd perform, wedging themselves like vines, leaves, wet
    flowers, into a swampy pattern so inanimate

    they fooled even the leanest panthers. One day they agreed
Point A was a mine full of tunnels here and there. How giant insects are
    they noticed too late and only then, poor remnants.

Fringe People
—for Ruth Yorck

How to tell fringe people from yourself, himself, us, you, her?
They hunt for central beds full of lovers to deceive.
When they enter rooms, the most valuable still-life shatters.
They scream "Trap!" deliberately trip (won't get up, ever leave).

Thus their Hollywood looks get damaged. Forced to aim at
Invisibility, they hide for hours, hood for weeks. Oops, there they are!
Caught pulling at their lips, they form the Pro-Compassion League.
Dreadful clowns, their motto: for every laugh a scar.

Their latest? "Get centered is our this year's mystique.
Our ideal of haven is a hurricane's eye, a calm norm
And to hell with the others!" Verbatim. Alas their mask
Even inches away looks like perfect skin and their smile, ah warm!

Halloween Loop

awaiting arrest
sky-high nonchalance
walk on by (off orange girder)

comely comedy
construction workers agog
they laugh: hey Mack

their helmets
(my new charm device: *sera sera)*
silver streaks against the black

night now
someone's drug death's my doing
my umpty-umpth dream murder

warm day
metal shop grills clank open
along the Medit . . . the Pacif . . .

frontal horror
"most people are dead on their feet"
turn page

it's Edwin Denby
Ronsard and I must part forever
it's that kind of wrap-around age

yank off all the knobs
well all reet!
nod off, nod off, as if . . . as if . . .

Nov 25

toy bird on its back one metal wing now broken
once tottered tempo arthritic spastic

along an El sidewalk in a Fifties home movie
featuring a clean-cut boy version of Ashbery

gazing sexily at sparrers in a gym with open windows
the express gathers momentum and now you see

Frank O'Hara walking on the tracks suiciding supposedly
John Latouche the bird's winder-upper died first

and soon after I turned into a "baby poet"
inventor of the read-a-curved pretzel ocean moon hands

a slight delay while the ribbon expands
the breakage around this desk is something fierce

dumb how the object all too often outlasts the person
all too often not counting art shoot why count art he gagged

a testy insight due to the aging process repeat aging process
skipping breakfast always puts me in a confessional mood

frankly I began this poem day before yesterday
the title's a downright lie more so by the minute

especially as this poem's been festering let's see
since I lost that toy car in the black space under the house

my first memory (dirt) the victrola's running down
and that witch in the tree outside is waiting to strangle me

frankly this poem started to be about a photo Nov 25
Nixon's shoes being shined front-page Nov 25

two shoeshine boys bent way way down Nov 25
freak-out overtones of foot kissage

leading to clompy polkas of national ass lickage
of great beefy men on red leather thrones

in a marble station yellowed with—looks like
hippies have been dropping stuff on the cops again

the soft-drink industry must be ecstatic anyway
meanwhile us good guys are stalled in the Tunnel of Fuzz

"stuck my dong up the Great Speckled Hawg
them glinty shiny flecks was molybdenum zinc"

the lights just came on again all over the world
a slight decay while the ribbon gets some rest

some deep-freeze therapy for us women and kids please
and when we come back up and the tundra starts to fizz

with our secret oral teachings (psalm one: city lights)
we'll wrap our bombed friends in palm fronds

and become a singing people (did you enjoy your turkey?)
hey we *are* a singing people (the wing part tasted metallic)

Awake on March 27th

my thoughts turn up
always the first one up around here
Ted's god-fearing farmer red Hi Folks beard
with its growth of unabashed pseudo-pubic hair
mebbe's scratching kinkily against the clean maiden
sheets as pellets of old speed sift through his system
asleep on top floor

asleep on third floor
the flu sleeper
judging from Joe's shifting hot metal body parts
you'd think he was a jalopy in the tropics
making heat noises in the cool moonlight
clicks out of sync with the silver moonlight
only it's dawn
another hot red day
my thoughts turn south
fly away from spring
the city's about to unloosen its stays
all-around relentless blam-di-blam budding

asleep on second floor
white whippet with beige areas
(antarctic map)
cool nose come summer
end of sleepers list

yesterday empty excursion bus parked outside
babble babble ma and pa duck pat of butter daily
twenty years problem of month adds 165 pounds

Missing Persons to your Easter weight Easter weight
in place of street space a wall of bus windows
scary to come downstairs staring into bus

empty motor running empty stretched out on backseat
man face up corpse-gray uniform
end of sleepers list

First Frost

walk up to sunset pasture
autumn wonderland of milkweed floss
its spewing out frozen

in mid-free-fall
much as that summer stopped
fragments and remnants

returned to NYC
scared I'd wake up in DOA City
holocaust: no Frank O'Hara

audible chasm: no Frank O'Hara
snatches of his voice in certain intonations
blotting out process

no red leaves left
ritual: wrapped him in a rug
best dance we ever danced

song: on Dial-a-Poem
life two/thirds over ("grass" floss: frozen)
before I heard Frank sing

from

Album

White Attic

The white attic rests
among dripping trees

with unrolling tunnels
and trembling luggage

around were dens
all kinds of dens

and dazzling fruit
to weary the wind

the sun would end
and we'd smoke among the trees

our wary arms
tenderly relaxed

the urn faces a tree
of unequal height

when it came I grew
moved to two rooms in town

where I reach out at night
and bat the far air

Four Scenarios

■ I ■

MY HEART IS CALLING

The poor opera company

    adios
    South America

has reached that secret age

    rain in
    Monte Carlo

when all denouements seem tiresome

■ 2 ■

THE PHANTOM LIGHT

Gordon Harker of the North Stack Lighthouse
and Higgins his nervous accomplice
have the self-same sickness—
the need for adventure,
and here they are seen with Binnie Hale
dredging for "ice" in the lagoon.

    Now they pull the levers
    at the Great South Fair.
    The bridge sparkles, fragments.
    Captors tumble through the air.

▪ 3 ▪
TRIPLE TROUBLE

a trunkful of rifles
to force the Premier . . .

drunk in a fog
the family (it's winter)
have an inter-family row

who'll tell the boy
with the glass-breaking complex
how the silk underthings
were found on the dunes

▪ 4 ▪
THE MEMORY EXPERT

America's greatest showman
injures his hands in an accident

the hands of a guillotined murderer
are grafted on by Yvonne

fortune smiles on their marriage
and every show they produce

an uncanny lust to throw knives
enlivens their jungle safari

America's greatest showman
wills her a wealth of red hair

Aztec Dinner Dance

The hogstore bogus couple
sprayed their bonus verandah of steel net mesh
with mahogany, maps, and a little wire studded in places.

Aztec Dinner Dance Tonight
came through the tube just sprayed with granitic follicles
to deter the youngsters from inhaling so much.

And what of their home?
The garden spray had finished up wetting the wall
and now was drenching some flowers and a rainbow.

Aztec Dinner Dance Tonight
came through the tube as Aunt Grass sprayed it
with putrid motes to deter the family decadence: random sniffs.

Olé the floating islands
managed their pavane
tastefully bumping like vague turtles.
Some strange mountains
lumbered into the garden,
languidly embracing while night parrots moaned.

A silly atmosphere
greeted Mount Popocatepetl.
Then the forgivable rush of pine surfaces, avid,
sparks and gashes,
the pain of new chasms in the zodiac.
They sprayed a little, and hummed around the red ruins.

"That was the loveliest spray of them all,
dumping ancient milk out the window."
She pulled up the covers, and that was how she went,
whirred into invisibility.

Aztec Dinner Dance Tonight
came through the tube. And how she would have wanted it.
But what of us and our processions?
South? Further South? South?
No. Let us shamble back North. Back North.
East and West lie black posts in the hot sky,
guides anyway.

Revolutionary Letter

The pulp magazine lay there, dangling sloppily, two-thirds, etc. Flat etc. Piled high etc. with typically ugly etc. New Jersey roadside situation etc. In the fissures, cockroaches were peering out, lined up to enjoy the sunrise and the distant orange-flecked towers of the futuristic city. All chunked out in an obvious way—irregular shapes, linear in a tilty way. All chunked out in an obvious way. Just what'd appeal to a stenographer clomping around in wedgies, fidgeting with her baby-pink snood with one hand, and with the other trying to finish the orange popsicle before it melts in the sun. What a telltale trail on the sidewalk—it skirts the pale blue plastic doily with the marzipan of the trumpet hearing aid centered on it, on the curb next to the person on the stretcher in the gutter, surrounded by young people in green smocks, trainees probably. The stenographer is shouting at her, time for the news and the weather—please come home! The orange liquid has wetted the doily. The person's fingers are so agitated! Sign language? One of the smock people is interpreting—proceed to the corner, garden apartment, the newspaper, walk back to the griddle, potato pancakes—sticky fingers from maple syrup. She can't stand sticky fingers. The inferior paper napkins sold nowadays shred easily—and however patient and careful one may start out being—one is soon sawing the air with abrasive gestures. Surely the interpreter is elaborating somewhat. The person has a good, simple face, although its spirituality may be accented by the closed eyes. The interpreter is shouting about "blocks" etc. "Lumps." "Excess material cluttering up the new declivities—it's so rusty from the increasingly difficult-to-predict storm patterns. One can't move them into the sheltered areas due to the snarled mobility sequences . . . nothing goes by . . . the metal piece must be moved ten yards . . . serrated edges that can do unquestionable physical damage

. . . a veritable onrush . . . dyed blonde harridans with baby carriages laden with groceries . . . big meaty men in vicuña coats, forming a flying wedge. "Lumps." He simply refuses to say the word "chunks"—all chunked out in an obvious way. Irregular shapes, linear in a tilty way. All chunked out in an obvious way. So obvious!

Breech Baby

I was a Breech Baby. My mother was warned
against having me as she was in her forties, and
her health was none too good. She was of U.S.
Hungarian-Germanic-Jewish-White-Southerner
Protestant
extraction.

Now comes the important part. The doctor reached in her and
flipped me over with his hand, so I came out, but how I don't
know, for now she's dead. The doctor is also dead. My father
is also dead. All my aunts are dead. And my uncles. The hos-
pital is torn down. In its place is a park where nannies wheel
their charges, cooing lullabies, and bearded men in bowlers
take out their solid gold watches to see if their lunch hour is up.
It is a nicer city now.

Now comes the important part. We left the city for our home at 1914 El Parque in
Colorado Springs seven weeks later. Everyone was carrying hooch in their
picnic hampers and suitcases—ah, Prohibition! We all formed a massive spiral in the
station. The redcaps stared, and covering their mouths with their hands, laughed
at the sight of this wrinkled red blob with a wizened face (me!) being borne aloft.

Now comes the important part.
The family consisted of:

ranch-rattlesnakes-Popsy-polo-flags-Menzo-blood-
Ramona-Broadmoor-Edna-cough-swing-Zenobia-

MZ (a) — Moom
MZ (b) — Doogi

zoo-cough-dawg-bluffs-was-English-hoss-tequila-
Vivi-Cici-hernia-Packard-beadwork-

mz (A) — Soos-voo (1)
mz (B) — Soos-voo (2)

sled-hobo-King-sneezes-attic-sidewalks-cherries-
rabbit-backboard-Wagner-attic-Denver-Parcheesi-

mz (a) — Noo (a)
mz (b) — Noo (b)

Belinda-choker-bike-Diana-Oz-Bojangles-
saddle-pool-Guy-witch-pee-speedometer-

Paper Suns

Gordon makes abusive telephone calls. Uncle Charles pulls over to the side by an inn. He gets out of the car and dies. Gordon comes to the funeral and walks in the garden but does not set foot in the house. Ken takes up the crusade! He avoids introducing her to his future wife. She sends two chairs as a wedding present. Mervin thinks that with so much china in her house, she should write him—use all you want, take all you want. His partner is killed in the war. The papers proving ownership of the properties has been transferred are lost. The money is totally lost. Bill goes to a prep school where he wins scholarships. From there to Cambridge, where he studies law. He is hired out to an agency as a tutor. He forgets to take his name off the rolls! He goes to Paris with a money-belt strapped to his waist. The yacht sets sail and turns around in midstream. Land boom in Canada! He goes there. He becomes a useful foil. Edith whirls from one diplomat to another, and uses him to keep off too ardent swains. He is an eccentric who really is not eccentric. He never quite makes a go of his life. Some people lose sizable sums, which he never pays back or regards as his fault. He quarrels and goes off to make munitions. To be on his own? To do something for his country? The banks fold. "Where shall we eat, honey?" Mary bets Bill that Constance's five dollar gold piece will not be accepted. On a hillside he says, "We'll make you Manageress." She asks Constance if he's serious. Constance says, "Oh, no. It only gives him something to talk about." She spends hours on the phone. Alice and Mary come over. Gordon moves. Kenward won't go on the same train. He gets up earlier and comes home later. This goes on for a year. "Why not let him make his own friends, lead his own life?" "The money. I haven't the money." Doris never signs a check. Once a week, she accounts for everything spent. Kenward goes to Nigeria. Gordon begins to die. He never gets over the shock. Something is knocked out of him.

Poem Songs

Air

sight
impinges
on air

divvying it up
night sky
into a cup

black earth
(good omen)
full of mica

suspended overhead
it's July
I'm full of joy

no steam heat
no cream teat
no dream meat

just walking around
watching the cup
dump its load

right on my head
cool black jelly
full of glints

hints
to remind me
of air

Bio

Scratch   NYC old guru
Don't rent me out as a mosquito detour   ooh

            Non   want
            Geritol,   Vermont

        From crazy brat reading Krazy Kat
        To Kafkaesque this Kafkaesque that

Never saw "action"   ransacked my dance act
Came up with   a nance act

            Trek   aids
            Sped up the decades

            Loved   ones
            Re-re-re-re-re-re-re-reruns

        Full of   blubbery residents
        Watching rubbery Presidents

And me, the figure in the carport, the proverbial carport
Unrafeened Laff Fiend   dreaming of a far port

Of Chinatown torsos and fizzes
What   is is

Fields   unfenced
Tomato plants to brush against

Heliotrope
Dope

A whiff   tease
From the Fifties

Went around   in a fib haze
Never went through a lib phase

My whippet wants in   is in
Keeping tabs on bug-bite scabs   sniffs at my skin

Eggs

Though I'm not a woman
Falling in love overnight
Leaving nothing for the children to quarrel over

L   equals the old El, rattling through my dreams.
O   equals multiple-choice olive grove.
V   equals vicuña, we snuggled over and under, got shredded.
E   equals eggs in the morning, easy over.

> Scrambled eggs.
> Deli eggs.
> Smelly eggs.
> Morass.
> Bus depot eggs.
>
> Grease-monkey always smiling,
> Up at me, eating my eggs.
> On my pants.
>
> Field, dinosaur eggs.
> Flyin' down to Rio.
> Handsome. Huevos.
> G'wan. I can't decide.
> Dawn. Sunny side up.
>
> Showered at the Y.
> Second balcony.
> Rooftop. Back of truck.
> Scrambled egg sandweeeech.

Oeuvres. Gallery eggs.
Bogotá. Dried wartime eggs.
Car. Rented car.
Hotel eggs. Motel eggs.
Motel eggs. Hotel eggs.
Harlem. Boxcar.
Yachts riding out the storm.

Eggs on the rocks. Crack.
Sleep. Cracks.

Bed. Bed eggs.
Sleep eggs closing out intruders.

Sin in the Hinterlands
—for Gerrit Lansing

'Grashulations,
Fingerprint Man!
Then rush rush.
Slip off white covers—
Simple home ceremony,
Foto.
Foto-rinse.
Foto-bins.

Then home.
Climb into padded think trunk.
Wait for burble of ancestry info:
Bio.
Canned info bio.
Canned bio logo
With Daffy Duck forefinger blur.

Told you so
(Spinster)
Told you so.
No foxtrot,
Luxury of foxtrot,
Foxtrot dip,
Dip gimp of Valhalla.

Dick fun tone of voice
Stalled between floors.

A simon-pure energy vestige.
Kaput, get it?
Another solid blue day
Of role reversals;
Healthy sun,
Sick wisp kaput—
Like a sex act cordoned off
In the silliness
Of a reflecting pool.

Malarial feel about things.
People in charge long since gone.
Where's the stamina
Outpost life thrives on?

Lip-sync.
A life of lip-sync.
It's like a life of lip-sync—
Lip-sync of tip of vat. Hot vat.

To help maintenance of upsurge—
    Tree. An up.
    Bluejay squawks.
    Nubbin doodads.
    Tree turning upside down.
    Imbedded birds.
    Dormant cornucopia.

      Freeze it.

Bang-Bang Tango

Me and my giant orangoutang doll.
And now you.

Me and Jim-Merv-Val.
The poil of the Palais Blau Taj Mahal.
And now you.

> Tango zat Bang-Bang Tango
> Zat Bang-Bang Tango
> Bang-Bang.

Me and those boxes of demitasse spoons from classy hotels,
All she left behind, and she left them to me,
Ma chère Marguerite.
And now you.

Me and Heidi, my miniature chow,
Eat up the puppy-dog, bow-wow,
Eat up the pussy-cat, meow-meow,
Eat up Baby Bebe, vite!
Wah-wah! Eat! Eat! EAT!
And now you.

> Tango zat Bang-Bang Tango
> Zat Bang-Bang Tango
> Bang-Bang.

Me and Alfredo's pneu:
Molti Soldi Goombye Old Bag Olé.
And now you.

Me and my favorite metropolis,
Oslo in April, la la,
Then on to Reykjavík, eek,
Oompah-pah!
Where Papa Gump and I
Tasted real snowflakes in May,
Only last May . . .
And now you.

      Tango zat Bang-Bang Tango
        Zat Bang-Bang Tango
          Bang-Bang.

Me and my butterfly dance
For the man in dark glasses
Who whispered, "No cherce, got no cherce."
And I ran, bang-bang,
And I sang, bang-bang,
Orangoutang, bang-bang,
"Got no cherce, got no cherce . . ."
      And now you.

Me and my déjà vu
Of a fidgety midget delivery boy
Unzipping my lily-white chilly white shroud,
Sinking back with me in a horse-drawn hearse.
      Aye! It's YOU!

      Tango zat Bang-Bang Tango
        Tango zat Bang-Bang
          Tango zat Bang
            Tango zat.
              Zat.

Sneaky Pete

What's happened to the poem as poem, Sneaky Pete?
What's happened to the poem as poem?

    It's crossing the Pacific
    In an underwater sky lab,
    In a cute little butane box
    In a gizmo way down there.

    And the shitty air smells pretty
    To us old-time gringos,
    But our loop-the-loop-the-loop biplane
    Isn't used to the tundra.

    So push a little harder
    Till the gizmo acts frisky
    With multi-colored fissures
    That widen as you walk.

Rush-hour joggers brush against me
Whispering of nightmarish accessories.

What's happened to the poem as poem, Sneaky Pete?
What's happened to the poem as poem?

    It's dangling from a black hole
    In a Golden Oldie time warp,
    In a fun little gunnysack
    In a doodad way up here.

Yin. The cute die in summer.
Yang. Dark out and the curtain's stuck.

There's a Papa Doc sunset
On my "That's All, Folks!" burnoose.
No touchee! Its naked loins
Turn young lungs puce.

Jes' keep your lips on the siphon, hon.
I'm movin' back to town.

Back where the poem as poem's gone,
Back where the poem's gone.
Back where the poem as poem's gone.
Back where the poem's gone.

And I Was There

That symbiosis in the garden
Says to adventure.
The jelly on the daffodil
Will mildew by July,
And the orange result
If the birds come by
Will suffice as our capitol, won't it?

And I was there. And I was there.
And I was there. And I was there.
            And I was there.

Here we are, in what seems to be
An ærial predicament.
The Government certainly looks handsome
In the mackerel sky,
Awaiting wind fungus
Beribboned in its way, good-bye.
Blackamoor stump,
How luminous you'll be.

And I was there. And I was there.
And I was there. And I was there.
            And I was there.

Adele The Vaudeville Martinet

Naked but for golden boots, she conquered Colorado.
Banjo expertise made whole beaches dream of wheat.
  "Avril, Avril" she sang
  And balanced balls of glass.

As Delia the Moppet, ten years she toured Havana.
Farmboys brought her ancient lace. Whole plazas tasted snow.
  "Avril, Avril" she sang
  And juggled knives of stone.

She gilt herself all over for the nightclubs of the north.
But the parrot dropped its flag, and the tourists talked of home.
  "Avril, Avril" she sang
  And sequins hid her icy eyes.

Meat

Our dumb city's on a Hallucinatory Map.
Ruby Buddha's are sucked off the breasts of—
Of   of   of   of   of   of   of   of   of   of
Of   of   of   of   of   of   of   of   of   of

And now the truth. They're platinum-colored plastic.
See those haunches? De Lawd marauding again.
        Against the wind.   Uh huh.
        Against the wind.   Uh huh.
              Huh.

Our bum city's known as Hallucinatory Trap.
Diamond stickpins are plucked off the vests of—
Of   of   of   of   of   of   of   of   of   of
Of   of   of   of   of   of   of   of   of   of

And now the truth. It's gittin' rather drastic.
See those haunches? Us riffraff, sniffin' again.
        Against the wind.   Uh huh.
        Against the wind.   Uh huh.
              Huh.

Our slum city's full of Hallucinatory Crap.
Zircon mood rings are chucked off the chests of—
Of   of   of   of   of   of   of   of   of   of
Of   of   of   of   of   of   of   of   of   of

And now the truth. It's really so fantastic.
See those haunches? De Daid parading again.
        Against the wind.   Uh huh.
        Against the wind.   Uh huh.
              Huh.

Girl Machine

my nerves my nerves I'm going mad
my nerves my nerves I'm going mad
round-the-world
hook-ups
head lit up head lit up head lit up
the fitting the poodle
MGM MGM MGM
MGM MGM MGM
MGM MGM MGM
the fitting the poodle

What a life just falling in and out of
What a life just falling in and out of
swimming pools
xylophones   WANTED   xylophones
WANTED   female singer   WANTED
bigtime floorshow   bigtime floorshow
bigtime floorshow   bigtime floorshow

Busby Berkeley
silhouetted in moonlight moonlight
silhouetted in moonlight moonlight
mysterious mirrors
mysterious mirrors
Gold Diggers of Blankety Blank
Clickety Clack   Clickety Clack
swell teeth   not news
swell teeth   not news
WOO-WOO   WOO-WOO
WOO-WOO   WOO-WOO
Gold Diggers of Blankety Blank
Clickety Clack   Clickety Clack

swell teeth
mysterious mirrors
mysterious mirrors
Busby Berkeley

shiny black surfaces
shiny black surfaces
shiny black surfaces

a girl machine
a girl machine

work work work   work work work
work work work   work work work
work work work   work work work
work work work work work

show gets on and is a smasheroo
show gets on and is a smasheroo
round-the-world
hook-ups

Busby Berkeley is the Albert Einstein
of the movie mu
Quantum Leap
Babe Rainbow
Girl Machine   Girl Machine
Quantum Leap
Babe Rainbow
Girl Machine   Girl Machine

reflected and refracted
by black floors and mystery meers
reflected and refracted
by black floors and mystery meers

Night in Shanghai
Night in Shanghai
Girl Machine   Girl Machine
Girl Machine   Girl Machine

lips painted red
Girl Machine   Girl Machine
Girl Machine   Girl Machine
keep on doing it
the oriental fans part

Girl Machine   Girl Machine
Girl Machine   Girl Machine
distant hands

Girl Machine   Girl Machine
Girl Machine   Girl Machine
they come nearer

Girl Machine   Girl Machine
Girl Machine   Girl Machine
harmonica player
Girl Machine   Girl Machine
Girl Machine   Girl Machine
falls for Jane Wy

Girl Machine   Girl Machine
Girl Machine   Girl Machine
pursued by gangs

carries her shot dead
Girl Machine   Girl Machine
Girl Machine   Girl Machine
down a shadowy dream corridor
Girl Machine   Girl Machine
Girl Machine   Girl Machine

an endless dream corridor
Girl Machine   Girl Machine
Girl Machine   Girl Machine
they get smaller
a shadowy dream corridor
Girl Machine   Girl Machine
Girl Machine   Girl Machine
distant hands
an endless dream corridor

Girl Machine   Girl Machine
Girl Machine   Girl Machine
down a shadowy endless dream corridor
the oriental fans close

42nd St   42nd St   42nd St   42nd St
42nd St   42nd St   42nd St   42nd St
reflected and refracted
by black floors and mystery meers
42nd St   42nd St   42nd St   42nd St
42nd St   42nd St   42nd St   42nd St
black floors and mystery meers

you in the view
and no real walls
you in the view
and no real walls

express flow
black whi   t
express flow
black   whi

firm shiny terror
express   flow
black   whi

firm shiny terror
express   flow
black whi

you in the view
and no real walls
you in the view
and no real walls

Girl Machine Girl Machine
Girl Machine Girl Machine
Girl Machine Girl Machine
Girl Machine Girl Machine
Girl Machine Girl Machine
Girl Machine Girl Machine

bunches like flowers
down the ramp
beautiful people working for us

Girl Machine Girl Machine
Girl Machine Girl Machine
Girl Machine Girl Machine
Girl Machine Girl Machine

happy factory
just relax

Girl Machine Girl Machine
Girl Machine Girl Machine
Girl Machine Girl Machine
Girl Machine Girl Machine

just relax
just relax

just

relax

relax

from

Motor Disturbance

Fruit

Oranges,
someday the Negress who smears you with certified color
will hear tap-taps and whines (the Giant Fruitbeast)
in the swamplands, arising like natural music,
and she will shriek in her swoon,
"American youth, go stomp on your car graveyards!
Small boys in acid underwear, once more you may yoohoo
at trains in the night. Whoo-ee, the alleys of Kansas
are now devoid of yellow joke eggs that hop peep and explode.
City children, accept the perfume of your melons in the sun—
                    Lemons."

Limes,
in spring you remind some men of little people's breasts.
Irish bodies—the huggle-duggle of many cellophane sacs—
or even the Indians on stilts who harvest government orchards
know: a lime on a turntable encourages the wrong voyagers.

Plop them into snowbanks, northern strangers, and in summer
when they roll onto roads, slovenly families at pasture
will remember to kick the cattle. Farm women in bed a-mornings,
think of them in your bureau, then get up. A nation of you and you,
                    Grapefruit,
                    Tangerines,
could only prove the all-nite cities have won. O lovely spring,
the carnage! Oldsters with blinky chicken eyes resent your seeds,
your sections, your juice and meats. Secretly in markets,
they pinch you, hurry on and sniff their fingertips, estranged.

The Dustbowl

The Harvey Girls invaded Kansas that spring of the famine
nudged by sweet memories of cornfields in the snow.
Okie weeders. Stranded in the orchards. Huts. Silos.

Ah, the times they had—huts—racing down avenues
of rattly stalks, droopy and sere, oooo-eeee! roughhousing
in jeans and poke bonnets until the laundry basin

announced supper (thwacked) beans and jello (thwacked)
followed by coupling in the sheds. Alas that winter of the famine
there were no sheds, and still they stayed, sullen

girls of the south, squinting at yellow skies
out of verboten shacks. Alas that summer of the famine
they breakfasted on leaves from gullies

and the air tasted of acorns, ah, the meadows smelled of vanilla.
Alas that winter of the famine, their men lay down on the highways
and their women lay down with them, and felt the hot truck wind.

Alas ladies in the cities, clutching their scalloped hankies,
oiled up the icy sidewalks in the violet dusk
and hitching up their leathern garments, fell and sued.

Taxes. Caverns. Cereal. Vegetate. Simple gestures
(entering attics, bikes wobbling, dogs sunning)
    lurched into something checkerboard, with every piece

    outsized, gummed to attract the police.
The Harvey Girls slept until came the spring of the glut.
    Thrumming, the weed machines released an ebony menace.

That summer of the glut, the fields were like monsters in heat,
and the Harvey Girls, freckled and worn, smiled at the northern mistral,
    and headed on mules for the mountains, that autumn of the glut.

History of France

Wind, cold, rain.
Then came the sky person:
a pale empress.

Today is beautiful—
such lively girls!
A sharp-cornered stone hovers.

Ah, rigid acceptance!
Money buys everything
Except walls between people.

The empire in the rain
with the muzzled atmosphere
stopped us at the border.

Striped barriers! Oafs!
And beyond, men in swimsuits shout,
"Art, make us free."

Another plaintive morning
full of chickens, dust, and buoys.
The sea keeps re-beginning . . .

Lobster claws in the pine forests
betoken an illogical sea
which sings: *I know, I know.*

Sticky tar and plastic messes
clarify the alliance of judge and guide.
True democracy need never exist.

Not only need, but never will.
Think of cliffs. Think of peacocks.
And the salty skiffs of the colonels.

Withdrawing rooms come next: perfumed earphones
for the young people—it's the Divine Sarah.
Wooden leg sounds bump about the divans.

"Secrecy in the provinces,
a journey under a waterfall—
these won't test your manhood, Robert."

A pretty woodwind, and thrushes.
They say the dormers fly open
to admit sweet-faced aristocrats.

And the maids dump out the cakes,
the pretty bush design on the main course,
while everyone hides letters in hollow trees.

The party includes the lady with the map-shaped face,
the boyish man, the chess-playing lifeguard.
How they love the French summers recently.

The cleverer towns have crested yellow parks,
nice and oblong with ferns and pebble deer,
and on these the old sweet lovers loll (the wasps).

Underneath them, musical flushing,
tunnels to the ocean,
and bloated hairy sea creatures.

We have never (bump) sat on (bump) rocks,
the women facing west,
and watched the Atlantic and Pacific sunset,

the men tucked into blankets,
the children tucked in too,
and the old people in the cars.

Well done! You see, the cities
have erected spangled circus nets
or are they nests?

Into them (keep whirring, pap factories!)
ocean souvenirs fall, misty bitchy things,
so the boulevards get more usage.

Now, in the mountain gravel pits,
the workers wear scoopy hats,
in which they smuggle out the granules.

But in the mauve valleys,
such attractive colleges,
all built on animal cemeteries, alas.

In winter they pack 'em solid,
come spring, to Hans and Ivan's amazement,
but now—he reaches the valuables:

fountains of exposed beasts and breasts,
lottery tickets in the sluices,
to prevent the acids from seeping through.

In the warehouse, racketeers
daydream of that sky person,
the pale empress.

At lunchtime, they take it out,
the tongue-shaped wooden box.
Today is beautiful.

Shirley Temple Surrounded by Lions

In a world where kapok on a sidewalk looks like an "accident"
—innards—would that freckles could enlarge, well, meaningfully
    into kind of friendly brown kingdoms, all isolate,
with a hero's route, feral glens,
    and a fountain where heroines cool their mouths.

Scenario: an albino industrialiste, invited to the beach at noon
(and to such old exiles, oceans hardly teem with ambiguities)
    by a lifeguard after her formulæ, though in love—
"Prop-men, the gardenias, the mimosa need anti-droopage stuffing."
    Interestingly slow, the bush and rush filming.

Hiatus, everyone. After the idea of California sort of took root,
we found ourselves in this cookie forest; she closed the newspaper,
groped past cabañas, blanched and ungainly.

The grips watched Marv and Herm movies of birds tweeting,
fluttering around and in and out an old boat fridge, on a reef,
when eek, the door, or was it "eef"? "Shirl" said the starling, end of

The janitors are watching movies of men and women ruminating.
        Then a cartoon of two clocks licking.
        Chime. Licking. Chime. *Then* a?
After that, photos of incinerators in use moved families more
        than the candy grass toy that retches. Dogs.
        For the dressers, *Mutations,*
about various feelers. For the extras, movies of revenge that last.

This spree has to last. "Accept my pink eyes, continual swathing,"
Shirley rehearsed. "Encase me in sand, then let's get kissy."
        Do children have integrity, i.e. eyes?
        Newsreels, ponder this.
How slow the filming is for a grayish day with its bonnet
        bumping along the pioneer footpath,
        pulled by—here, yowly hound.

The Power Plant Sestina

Horizon, burn with a smoky flame.
Thousands of women will bob up and down
left, right, left, and right, left, right.
Give me something pearl-shaped and soft
(like blue crystals) to offset hard work,
and don't forbid amber at the center.

At the center,
fossils flame,
and resins work
like jungle rafts moving down
evil-smelling rapids so soft
the rubbery leaves above look right.

How right
for embers at the center
steamy and soft
in an annual flame
to feel like down, warm down
on cheeks that never work.

Work, work. A world of work!
Dahlias! Zinnias! Give us this right!
Detention addicts, we bend down
and search for the center,
the glassed-in flame
that sifts tough from soft.

Terror makes us soft:
see how earthquakes work.
The example of flame
gives us the right
to choose the edge and abandon the center.
Watch it hurtle down!

Through a smoky sky, it'll hurtle down.
Instead, something pearl-shaped and soft
Will reconnoiter around the vanished center:
blue crystals to offset hard work.
Feel all right? Feel all right.
Protected from flame? Protected from flame.

Down goes the flame,
Soft-seeming and right
As the center of all work.

Japanese City

Centennial of Melville's birth this morning.
Whale balloons drift up released by priests. Whale floats parade
followed by boats of boys in sou'westers jiggled by runners
followed by aldermen in a ritual skiff propelled by "surf"—girls.
In my hotel room with its cellophane partitions (underwatery)
I phone down for ice water, tumbler, and the cubes.

Cattle for the Xmas market fill the streets.
Black snouts—a rubby day indeed. Bump the buildings, herds.
A Mexican seamstress brings back my underthings shyly
six, seven times a day. One sweats so, lying about.
She mentions marvelous pistachio-green caverns
where one canoes through cool midgy Buddha beards

where drafts of polar air sound like cicadas, where—
About the partitions. The other travelers seem—
There were beautiful hairs in the washbasin this A.M.—
thick, and they smelled of limes
(good, that jibes with mine—ugh!—)
but mine, how perverse! Form a hoop, you there. Mine,

mine smell like old apples in a drawer. Jim the Salesman
and his cohorts are massaging my feet: a real treadmill example.
They're in lawn decor, ether machines, nocturnal learning clasps.
And Jim? Plays cards in his shorts, moves black fish around.
Black houses, the capitol. Hotel chunks. Sky chunks. The squeeze:
green odd numbers—white air, amputations and eagles, respite.

Red even numbers: body sections, ocean sac, great beach.
Green even numbers: oval jewels, quicksand, haven behind falls.
Jim's stammer's contagious, zen smut about hatcheries in the 'burbs,
how the women in the canneries came down with the "gills"—
hence bathtub lovemakings, couplings in the sewers.
The ice water comes.

The room clerk's pate shines up through the transparent floor.
Soon sin couples will start arriving, and one-way mirror teams
and government professionals with portable amulets—
shiny vinyl instruments that probe and stretch.
Much visiting back and forth. Pink blobs. Revels and surveys.
Many olive eyes'll close in a sleep of exhaustion. More ice water!

The celebrants in metal regalia jangle and tinkle
moving past the red-roofed villas of the Generals,
past the cubicles of the nakeds and into the harbor,
past the glum stone busts of the Generals, sitting in the water.
Out they go, (Jim etc.) into the sweet emptied city, leaving behind
the red odd numbers untouched: pleasure beaches, monsoons, sun.

Jan 24
—for John Ashbery

take care keep in touch best wish for New Year
what'll it be: tango palace in banana republic

that's one of the luxuries of longish-term survival in NYC
thinking of smallness and walled-off sad little dumb little places

New Zealand was my first post-puberty country crush
how it welcomed me and my wonderful labor-saving devices

permanent waves strap-onable wings automats for the capitol
socialism I love you your housing weekends sandy-lashed settlers

first let me explain my "just room for one more" dread
picture-book of World War I mounds of about-to-be-buried corpses

sub-sub-sub-basement flashed by hours ago and still moving down
that Fu Manchu creep peering through the peephole is no super

judging from the lamasery teetering on the fez-strewn cornice
it's Albania and I'm to rescue poor dear dotty King Zog

milk-white victim hands are protruding out of the glacier below
hands that sprout bushy werewolf hair when the moon is full

electrolysis and gelatin capsules could keep these hands nice
the catch is the nation's lovelies'd grow freak mustachios

the clandestine crystal set lights up: you're #1 Commie, Anna
it's Roumania and Anna Pauker pushes off in the goat-cart

polemics polemics polemics she moans phuffle phuffle sigh
my first lady dictator whew that explains the butch hairdo

lucky she has me to brain the transmission key
in mid-enzyme-synthetic-organ-introjection hormone cycle

Anna wake up the transmission key is now smashed
Anna and Zog are playing bezique on the Blue Express

dance manual *pour moi?*
Anna rests her scruffy head on his shoulder

a solitary tear wends its errant way
skirting medal after medal

piranha are nibbling iron clouds above Tirana
their droppings—filings—scoot about the cobblestones

magnetized by distant word reverberations
(memo: keep ears to ground)

back to Anna and Zog in their sumptuous berth
(Praha München Paris)

see the green cube Anna in the mesh cooker unit
it's poking out its pterodactyl wings very over-soul, *hein*

its beak is caught Anna says taking hammer from handbag
it's probing its feathers for social parasites like us Zog joshes

Papillons d'amour Anna says swooning into a spoon position
her first dirty joke and they awoke thus in a bus in the Rockies

just as this morning we awoke in a spoon position
you and I

unfolded unthinkingly and dispersed
for another time's-up type day

Feathered Dancers

Inside the lunchroom the traveling nuns wove
sleeping babies on doilies of lace.
A lovely recluse jabbered of bird lore and love:
        "Sunlight tints my face

        and warms the eggs outside
        perched on filthy columns of guilt.
        In the matted shadows where I hide,
        buzzards moult and weeds wilt."

Which reminds me of Mozambique
in that movie where blacks massacre Arabs.
The airport runway (the plane never lands, skims off) is bleak:
scarred syphilitic landscape—crater-sized scabs—

painted over with Pepsi ads—
as in my lunar Sahara dream—giant net comes out of sky,
encloses my open touring car. Joe slumps against Dad's
emergency wheel turner. Everyone's mouth-roof dry.

One interpretation. Mother hated blood!
When the duck Dad shot dripped on her leatherette lap-robe,
dark spots not unlike Georgia up-country mud,
her thumb and forefinger tightened (karma?) on my earlobe.

Another interpretation. Motor of my heart stalled!
I've heard truckers stick ping-pong balls up their butt
and jounce along having coast-to-coast orgasms, so-called.
Fermés, tousled jardins du Far West, I was taught—tight shut.

So you can't blame them. Take head, turnpikes.
Wedgies float back from reefs made of jeeps: more offshore debris.
Wadded chewy depressants and elatants gum up the footpaths. Remember Ike's
Doctor-The-Pump-&-Away-We-Jump Aloha speech to the Teamsters? "The—"

he began, and the platform collapsed, tipping him onto a traffic island.
An aroused citizenry fanned out through the factories that day
to expose the Big Cheese behind the sortie. Tanned,
I set sail for the coast, down the Erie and away,

and ate a big cheese in a café by the docks,
and pictured every room I'd ever slept in:
toilets and phone calls and oceans. Big rocks
were being loaded, just the color of my skin,

and I've been traveling ever since,
so let's go find an open glade,
like the ones in sporting prints,
(betrayed, delayed, afraid)

where we'll lie among the air-plants
in a perfect amphitheater in a soft pink afterglow.
How those handsome birds can prance,
ah . . . unattainable tableau.

Let's scratch the ground clean,
remove all stones and trash,
I mean open dance halls in the forest, I mean
where the earth's packed smooth and hard. Crash.

It's the Tale of the Creation. The whip cracks.
Albatrosses settle on swaying weeds.
Outside the lunchroom, tufts and air-sacs
swell to the size of fruits bursting with seeds.

[85]

Fig Mill

As to that lady hiding in the closet
("Spring is here!" "Spring is here!")

it's only February and spring ISN'T here,
not here in this western locality.

Rich in history and Indian lore,
the street names follow the Generals.

Which reminds me of a cowboy
who all his life was a model,

a loathsome cowboy in a mobile home
Pressing against the glue-covered glass.

Surprised we haven't worn out our windowpanes,
windowpanes, windowpanes, using our binoculars.

This morning a flock of little pin sis-
kins flew in, the beautiful things,

made for the cool water,
and everyone took the hint

and moved away from the drinking facilities
ing and bathing facilities.

One of our guests is an elderly man
we always refer to as the monkey.

He sits in an old armless rocking chair.
Anyone know how to take out the noise?

Always a crowd to see the portrayals!
Bearing the well-known bundle in his beak

a model stork made straight for the house.
A notice reads "NO MORE, PLEASE!"

He climbed atop this man's shiny bald head
as if to say, "Out of my way! I need a drink!"

His bright red bib
completed the fib.

Seagulls circled overhead.
Time for bed.

No tidbits there—
just dead air.

Candlelight and kisses sweet
ediblize the toughest meat.

I write poetry and song lyrics.
Bix, let me know if you can hear.

We'll form a chain of friendship
but I need suggestions please.

Flowers and/or birds painted on whip-
cord, chicks and chickadees

working away at a sunflower seed
in the winter-rusty green grass.

Now a history of Valentines.
A woman in Worcester, Mass.—

First a list of things I want.
Pearl chips in fish bowls,

Pearl chips in bulb bowls.
Downtowns discontinued this product.

The policy approved by businesses today
is to suit production to employee.

Now a history of Valentines.
A woman in Worcester, Mass.—

Valentines were the passion of Esther's life,
but she lived and died unmarried.

Valentines were frowned on as "foolish notes"
and the sending of them was forbidden.

Esther called in her girl friend June
whose little caboose was Baby Beth.

June put a man on bathroom scales
in polka dot shorts looking over his tummy.

June put a golfer with a golf ball in a nest,
just to see how pretty they are underneath.

June wet her brushes in her mouth (tragic habit)
which led to her death by lead poisoning.

Times are hard on the Hi-desert,
studying visitors, flocks of mini-birds,

hanging upside down on the suet bags,
leaving in one grand rush.

Baby Beth, she too feels blue,
entertaining at a barbeque.

Yes, it's a small world I live in,
warning system quite unique,

a zigzag path with different squares,
Doves in the Window, Broken Star,

a zigzag path with different squares,
Umbrella Girl, Broken Star, the both.

Motor Disturbance

Could be inching my way across moth turbulence
(wrong country? Honduras?—No! No! Nepal!)
due to a motor disturbance in some itinerary program computer
that failed to take into account my aversion to hot weather decay

and my love of eternal white silence
the result of a motor disturbance of some solar slope
I keep sliding down thanks to my own personal motor disturbance
the one that makes me puff up and screech (dog stars)

when I'd rather celebrate a White Cliff Mass
with friendly co-innocents in a clean commune above the clouds
where I won't have to cerebrate how to—how to—rip up stuff
work-oriented ancients painstakingly mass-produced

in vast sheets of legible shimmering matter
inspired, don't you know, by a longitude-latitude motor disturbance
(Earth plunges into new electromagnetic black space field—)
exhausting! I can't control my current motor disturbance—

so clicky, soppy, so picky—like the one that led me to assume
"dysfunction" was Brooklynese for "wedding" (nervous laughter)
which prompted me to dial NERVOUS first thing today
seeing as my booster clock . . . burnt oasis . . . plastic goo

so much of it this time of—of—
the operator's voice was laden with irony
irony I have no time to savor
due to the motor disturbance of this end-of-year period

which seems to be hurtling down a sleety dynamo
throbbing with hallucinatory instructions
each syllable of which lasts out a year of its own choosing
thanks to a blessed motor disturbance in the Heavens

i.e. your lips, gills, hills, tips—
a very contemporary motor disturbance
as gorgeous as blue plates spinning and wobbling and falling
conjoining to form Sky, replacing the old peeling one . . .

■ 2 ■

Sometimes you must persevere in the face of a huge motor disturbance
that settles on a whole city's brain like a big black bowl
part of an everywhere-in-the-universe night
like the one I see when the two mountains wrestling each other lie down

which happened in my mind just as I careened into your arms by mistake
to wish you a half-gnawed ear (new motor disturbance, I hate you!)
to wish you a Happy New Year Times (got it right for once)
and Happy New Year Times is my favorite motor disturbance of all

next to you who can transform stalled traffic into a beautiful panora—
(never get to finish this word in this particular lifetime)
ma—ma—a mama of endless blinky fields with unicorns that honk
as they twine around each other with languorous etc.

thanks to a permanent motor disturbance
just like mine, like yours, like ours, like our ecstasy
the ecstasy we left our nation in our will
to help it shudder its way through its inventive mole-run

the one its machines invented due to their one great motor disturbance,
the one that was supposed to prevent all the others,
the others that make me unable to figure out why
there's not one motor disturbance in the January sky

     and in the winter air
     with you there
     everything in my life just seems to jell,
     farewell.

from

Tropicalism

Routine Disruption

going way back to dusty road
before cars, silent walkers

come to junction
avoidance of junction

run towards woods
green field gives way

hole, plummet into it,
new universe

exciting freshness and strangeness
the strains don't apply here

accidentally reborn
head home

Middle Class Fantasies

Escape from burning searing through froth
permanent veneers in transit
wobbling past obedience-trained choppers
through sliding panels
into eyes following you around the room
good likenesses if you like prune faces

Old Man upstairs juggling living brain
to perpetuate worthless codicils
twin lobes

worthless
worthless

dusty erosion mounds

All you want?
Never!

From Hay to Play City,
play money, I read you,
gay walky-talky night thoughts,
fucky sucky somnambulists playing
House Store Doc
recapturing pint-sized bliss in closets
in which slept the artist Chagall
the composer Stravinsky—
what year *is* it?
Stavisky.

There isn't much we can do
except get out of the way,

lie down on mottled eucalyptus leaves.
Birthday guests yackety-yack unconcerned.

In the lit-up department store window
widow with black hearing-aid cord
drooping out of mouth onto lap.

Briefcases—
men writing all over the plane.

We shall always remember
these days of happiness,
having wiped that dream from the drawing board.

    Chaos has one bonus,
    somehow prevents total decay.
    Frills that loomed major
    are reduced to a single focus:
    flashbulbs popping around
    an ill-conceived plant-torture episode.
    We have something on everyone,
    something that will sound better,
    like all fairy stories,
    after it stands the test of time.
    Subliminal fear goes unnoticed:
    rocket into sun.

Winter Life

That phosphorescence blooming like a white flower sky
in the winter morning night
is ice, lake ice.

Snow streaks,
V for Vermont checks,
mark the correct answer:
end of balmy rain.
Mottled with mini-craters,
squiggly gray germy wormy places,
huge armpit sweat patches show through:
work-in-progress
with black marble water edges

     then woods   fields   dirt road   dirt sky
     waterfall   facing a hillock   a house

with me in it
summer person turned winter person
up for the duration
of whatever snaggle-toothed trajectory lies ahead,
veering now this way, now that,
but mostly in, out, in, out, in, out,
like a restless pet that won't stay put,
its only goal piling detritus around the big feet
in-between chase scenes

    BONES   SEEDS

transmogrified into personal terms

    ZONE   *GUIDES*
    LONER   KNEES
    POMES   FREEZ

umbilical cord with fang marks, Keep This Side Up, wingéd phallus at end of chain, magic transparent tape, rubber, band, spectacles, dictionary, dictionary of, dictionary of clichés, cliché roughage regurgitated in a soughing attic, the attic of the mind, the will, the viscera, the lights, the Isles of Langerhans, on up and out into dossiers of the dead, misnomers, blanks, dust-ridden perspectives, backlash, inessentials tossed overboard, niceties that have become basics, more backlash, it was Death Week, the motels were jammed, roadhouses packed, tourist cabins piled like cordwood, all that invaluable black gunk blew away, flew over the expectant throng of spectators in the amphitheater-under-the-stars—hewn out of red rocks made of ersatz—

    Whatever became of ersatz?
    To wring one's withers.
    Whatever became of withers?

    Warning.
    Beware of the Blue Bore
    of the good old summertime.

The boy stood on the burning deck, monkey-face,
eating peanuts by the peck, monkey-face.

    Throwback throwaways,
    once off the assembly line,
    in sequence, out of sequence, no matter,
    must expect to get raked by the claws
    of the omnipotent vaulter,
    whose leprosy flakes coalesce in a trice,
    flick at window, pound on groin,
    pirouette along seam in sky,
        dream in guy,
        pal, gal, wahoo,
        underwater glugs.

John door opens. Stranger says I LOVE YOU and means it the way dream people do sometimes: forever. Dream of someone dead. Dream of strange apartment. Game gam, dream of. Test walk. Fear everyone'll notice permanent irreversible damage. Snorts and stomps on back-steps. Weirdo deer. Weirdo deer wants in. Morning tableau. Horse. Horse on lawn. Profile of strange horse on lawn. Stares at himself in side-view mirror, side-view mirror of empty Toyota. Empty Toyota. I guide Ralph Weeks of East Calais Vermont through my rooms in the city, gliding through silence in the city.

In real life, come mud-time,
insects pick their way around ungainly hulks,
in fœtus position, rusting in the sun.

What with so much uselessness crowding in,
taking up valuable crawl space,
facilities aren't what they used to be.
The air smells of shit.
Electric chair shit.

O ersatz withers,
moored permanently over the insomniac volcano,
encapsulated in a zeppelin sleep lozenge,
if only you'd settle down somewhere streamlined,
under a clean white counterpane,
a waif wearing skyscraper spats,
unmentionables, a berry field,
calmed down inside, apples,
corn, lovable, tarragon,
telling the trees apart,
particular changes,
horseradish,
stump.

We desire, yet fear this *set-apartness*.
Freud harangued the Popes about this,
lined them up in waiting rooms,
they fell into a coma,
the waters are still very roiled.

It's customary to this day
to open one eye mischievously part way,
speckled brown, downy nut-brown,
like those of newsboys,
circa 1910, The Midwest, queer,
only patinæd over with a viewing screen of smoky jelly,
a grid of multiple squares clicking away:

> sunset, skid marks, railroad bridge
> lit up like a diadem leading to the
> towers, reflections of passing steam-
> ships in the windows, icy grip of
> loudspeaker words in your ear.

An apropos story's making the rounds of us lounge lizards,
about how we revenge ourselves on the living
with ever deeper and wider silences,
wilder silences,
our subterfuges having become face.

Stranded is Scoutmaster Porky Pig
in mid-blizzard on flagless flagpole.
TV Jimmy, his own cub-scout, is home, warm,
watching *Gladly, The Cross-Eyed Bear* cartoons.

> Practiced paw tugs at soccer shorts.
> Hairy fists tighten on furry ears.

All of which yields up, inch by inch
to the weigher and grader and sorter of stones
The Writing on the WaWa.

I was brought up different,
in a velvety bunker, a webby dark place
far from confusions and contusions.
For company at night, twinkling grimaces flashed on:
ads.

      Hello, you.   I love you.
      Hello, you.
      I—
      I—

Whereupon a green liquid oblong lit up.
Mittel Europa thumped through the wall,
drag shows, *Settembre,*
jazz boats,
with pillows to muffle the harangues,
the Yangtze ever-widening.
I shuffled along in buckled galoshes,
sipping beef juice,
into the Toonerville Trolley of our funicular garden,
yodeling,
waving sideways (refugee-style)
at the avalanches
and at Popeye,
phthisis, is sick, was sick, Olive Oyl,
immediate family members
moving up and down
into enameled English sunsets,
through yucca.

Overloaded jet spirals down,
cargo: Mayan calendar steles spelling out DOOM
to some in little stick people strokes,
to others, spirals down, a fragile equilibrium,
spirals down, Greetings from the Guild,
the birthday, the climate, the day,
the night, the surroundings,
the house, the lake,
the particulars,
particulars that rescue one from old cheap shots:
peering through holes of moth-eaten parachute
at lava balls heading for windshield,
spiraling down.

       All white.
       Underwater wall hidden.

       Melted in the night.

           Gray water.
           Balmy rain.

           Ate some kale.
           Some snow fell.
           Rehardened.

           Left. Came back.
           All white.
           Left.

Visual Radios

The gigantic ghost scissors clacked away at the Olympic Team on the glacier—youngsters engrossed in their summer beverage. Screened by sandy lashes, their eyes vanished under their upper lids, up, up. Slick but not *quite* right: maimed buck look. But that's what comes of years of flopping down anywhere, California-style: new professions zinging past, combinations and possible combinations that make you drool (gasp) aghast. Dumb come-on, none-the-less—to bank on the built-in climax that comes from realizing the death seizure is just a simulated orgasm moue.

Had to add screech-of-brakes, a shadowy forest for the secret police in black raincoats, alternating with white stone streets (parched Old World.) One-to-one visual ratio teeters. The stone streets take over. Shutters bang shut, doors slam like crazy, inside locks click. Some outrage no civilized person wants any part of is about to be committed. A monster must be loose.

Climbing into my bathrobe is like putting on a window. Two windows, to be exact—one front and one back—a window with just enough "give" for one's body contours—a window with regular panes. Blue sky view. It's two (sundial). The bride has confetti in her hair and veil. The yuppy groom must have a sweet tooth—he's sneaking white icing into his mouth behind her back. In the distance, pyramids. Big statues of watchdogs form a circle around everything. So much vastness in one fell swoop, desert vastness, makes me want to cry when I look at it reflected, having sandwiched myself between two mirrors.

Good. The maintenance men—rhinestone studs on their boots, monicker studs—are flushing out the Feeder Tubes with their mouths. The gland extracts should be coming through any second—front and back. The little teat wants more, more! Yaow! Ruff, ruff! Now its twin wants more too. Fair is fair, but, new feeder sequence inserted, they've packed up their gear. No more severed arteries today.

Shutters bang open, doors too. The whole slaphappy town is pouring out into the streets. Some delirium no civilized person would touch with a ten-foot pole has just been set into motion. The scissors must have savaged the monsters on the glacier.

Time Lags

Good to be back in the big city, bounding around the room, starkers. 348 ½ days to follow. Winter moon about to go behind skyscraper. You can hear its phones ring all summer long, the skyscraper the helicopters skim on and off of, jampacked with decision-makers, decision-reversers, and decision-avoiders, night and day, making the room shudder. My St. Bernard is exhausted from crawling under and back out from under the waterbed. 348 ¼ days to follow. By my rube-night-silence-backwoods climate clock, summer's long overdue.

Especially as summer was so . . . so . . . pfui. Gesündheit. And the one before that while normal in some respects . . . ochre clouds enveloped the patches of greensward. Afro wig assembly line (a sky tune) . . . sprouting out of the dust . . . milkweeds in the road . . . wasps with Etruscan warrior masks . . . orange chameleons . . . the sequential boxy set-up of the seasons, a habit pattern deeply ingrained since early childhood, based on the reward system, was no more. Noi doi-doi. Apii-nah-yah. Yah, a likely story, yah, but it happens to be true. Boxy set-ups, like treasure maps with wind cherubs, and clustered around each map—

landlubbers, full of nowhere-else-to-go pathos—their ups, their gowns, their smells, their mounds—waiting for a bed-time story that'll start authoritatively and trail off—just the way modern myths do—leaving an apologetic clue here, an apologetic clue there: EXHIBIT X—curlicues in the sand, nasty scuffle among the dune granules, involving some sub-species we needn't concern ourselves with at this particular stage in our development—EXHIBIT Y—scrap of elastic underwear used as a bookmark in a dog-eared copy of Proust (not that it matters, but is it male or female underwear, because it's my copy of Proust—mine, MINE!), EXHIBIT Z—so far back it may be only a memory of a memory of something someone blabbed about that I've come to accept as something I really did: a sugar cube centered on a round table, centuries pass, one hugs a tree, lavishes love on it, hanging on for dear life, more centuries pass, one slogs through a swamp, masked wasps whirr and stare, it's summer in the boxy days, a human panther girl, a fecund creature to me now, lies down beside me to stare up at a tunnel of pine-branch webs—one is strewn about, it's me all askew, like a bee in freezing weather—crawling around a flashing DON'T WALK sign—hunting for nectar. Still on Arroyo Time, he refuses to head home for some shut-eye, even though the winter moon has just emerged. 348 days to follow, hint hint.

Coda

The sun, goddamn thief, has dusted my face with the orange rays of its orange days, a free cosmetic that cracks and peels skin, is cracking and peeling my skin while I sit here in the dark, wondering what to do next, using up my last matches in my putt-putt, in the main watermain under Main Street, USA. Somewhere down there is The Champ, frolicking under old conduits amid the stench of lizards. The sunlight, goddamn thief, must have implanted him with gills.

Tropicalism

Ate orange.
Legs stained . . . stains turn into fur patches . . . fur patches
turn into puma hide . . . palaver re escape route . . . boy's lips . . .
chicken feather along outer perimeter of lower redder one with
up-and-down wrinkles fly is negotiating . . . too much pursing
. . . spooky profiles peer sideways on high-rise balconies . . . just
dummies so the gov't'll think everyone's home.

. 2 .

More palaver: antebellum. One lays one's smock on the griffin.
Siesta after a Technician Feast of foie gras washed down with
Grapette. Siesta leaning agin' the Michelangelo Adam—cold
muscles agin' which one rubs: no guards to be afraid of. Gosh,
how did they trundle him here? Via those new erosion lines
along the orange-red rivulets coursing beside the highway.
Clump of bad-mannered executives from the South, i.e. "North"
by local mental gymnastics . . . a real fresh new "North" full
of fresh new "executives" from even farther "North" . . . they
really model themselves on penguins . . . experts at survival
—camouflage-proud . . . waiting under trees with leaves that
hang down like exhausted elephant ears, waiting for the rain to
stop so they can motion for the flotilla disguised as a parrot
parade float, with its ack-ack measles pellets that sound like
someone sucking a stone teat. Ack-ack-ack-ack!

. 3 .

Just have to wait till the situation is more human. Coated with
mud, massive anxiety attacks—vapors, zinc, can of *petits-pois*,
zinc, vapors, zinc, can of *petits-pois*, zinc, *petits-pois*, etit poi,

titpo, it p, t. In the steam room, a friendly Texan haw-haw. Iced drinks sent in, two pink pillows with flamingo feathers inside, everyone oils up, lotta give-and-take (Embassy jerks) about lore.

■ 4 ■

They have two white-leaved vines, twining around the Warrior Tree, which the men ingest the bark of daily, so as to develop their *stren't*. Also killing tree. When tree dies, so does Chief. Walks off into the jungle. Some cross-dress in woman-ish fur-pieces, secrete beads under rock, join with neighboring tribe as Chief's "priestess-bride." No one can touch priestess privates, real bad magic see his dong. Doesn't exist. So he has pick of women. That's really something: guilt mechanisms function in 100% screwball way. So he has pick of women! Chief's religious duty to fuck him up ass. While, ouch, he's *in flagrante*—he's (belief) in trance communion with this tribe's Warrior Tree—knows whether to attack other tribes or not, how, when. He says ATTACK! So they do. Victory! Meta-morphosis: he becomes Chief Twin, eventually means big trouble. One-to-one fight using two sticks. Poison on end of one stick. Up to Resident Chief's #1 Wife to hand out the sticks. If she digs new Chief Twin, he's in like Flynn. Poison, by the way, not fatal. In fact, it's leaf-drug which elevates the defeated chief into magic state. Fly like bird. Swim like fish. Climb vines like fast bug. Ends his days revered Prophet. Food and love offerings daily, as he sits cross-legged at the door of his stilt hut. Dies. He's carried to top of Warrior Tree by stal-wart youths and pulleys in a Basket of Eternity & Rain. He sits in a raft made of pelts tied to balsa, and there he's set on fire. Ashes eaten by entire tribe, one flake per person, wrapped in raw vine leaf. Two sacred vines planted by Resident Chief. Time begins again. Year One.

▪ 5 ▪

...but ice is like a ray sleeping...I sobered up to certain pesky circumstances. How to stave off the hierarchic patterns that really maim, reduce them to a few ingratiating scars on my Halloween Kit harelip?

▪ 6 ▪

By staving off the mysterious death of Architecture as we know it, I cheated myself of an empty contentedness. Yes, the suite was full of necessities. Tinting spansules is a profession, yes. Disconcerting, but true. But what about the statue in the hall outside, peering through the glassless transom? Who is this HORST?

▪ 7 ▪

The authorities here are highly susp—SHUSH! OK TAKE THIS DOWN. Ché is going into market research—more relevant than doctoring the poor. OK TAKE THIS DOWN THEY DON'T GIVE FLYIN' FUCK. Every life saved broadens the base of the population pyramid that much more, until its substrata—slimy and fetid but with more energy than "thin-out" line near top—OK TAKE THIS DOWN AMIGO, OK? Roaches, tarantulas, roaches, tarantulas: in convoys of ten each, they hurry along the traffic lane marked with day-glo dots, and down the starveling's throat. The Big Divvy according to the (TRANSMISSIONITA PROBLEMAS AMIGO BEAR WITH ME)—in the fields at low enough level to circumvent the inevitability of mechanization taking command (SORRY PAL DIFFERENT FEEDER CHANNEL FOR NONCE— ERRATUM: NUNS) in which case the population pyramid (TOO- DLE-OO TIME WE GO UNDERGROUND AGAIN) will be restruc- tured as an obelisk, squeezing the hierarchy into a more nakedly vertical pattern that makes it impossible for the elite to reproduce themselves in sufficient numbers—less intermingling, less sloppy pecking-order in-fighting, more intra-bureau phoning, more non-destruct memos, more solitude at one's booth to which one is assigned early in life, but this obelisk isn't practical yet (HI BACK AGAIN C'EST MOI)—pyramid has years to go as long as its base keeps widening (say) five percent per annum—then its weight is sufficiently defused to reduce the rate of sinkage to (say) ten percent per annum, which gives us (say) oh, 2050 may be a bit mucho and the pyramid may have to be converted into a rectangle—sarcophagus with the lid hooked from the inside to cut down on hanky-panky (NO NEED TAKE REST DOWN MESSAGE OVER BYE-BYE)—golf pro has yen for daughter, not her flabby henna mama—only daughter and school chum—gov't censor demands X numero pesetas leave in snatches throbbing, with one girl tracing on other girl's boob—*CHÉ*—invisible finger-writing. Audience assumes it's *AMOR*—except for politics buffs.

▪ 8 ▪

Regular paintings in front of the arch with the discreet black curtain. Most interesting, that hard glare beating down on the lilies (Utrillo), with the ballerina Electro-Mix Maestro (Duchamp) floating over the Tudor bed and its inviting sateen spread, reflected in the mirror, and the teenage couple in the background, their bodies lightly touching, staring at the dawn from the balcony. They've been talking all night, you can tell, because they're Romeo and Juliet, and they have a great many lines to get through without any mistakes, and what with the trix of authentic pronounciation, and the subyunctive teensies coming at them so fast—

▪ 9 ▪

Men working high up, suspended on big wooden crates. Night shifts all over the city, finishing up white high-rises—before next onslaught of boondockers arrives, getting in on the proverbial ground floor.

▪ 10 ▪

Ché is so trusting re "Truth and Consequences." Too Yanquified. He has dreams of pressing flesh with Nixon in native village. They go in one, light toke, just sit there. Pow! Nixon is converted! He brings the brass, light toke. They're converted! Big Ten Day Speech to the U.S.A. Must stop "exploiting" etc. Impeached, natch. Chaos! Village? Corpse smoke rises from distant chimney. Bumblebees crawling around the empty Bumblebee tuna can.

▪ 11 ▪

Racial memory last night of a facial memory. Of an infinite number of taps—raindrops on leaf for months, months—that go into making a stone more cushion-like when one drapes one's back across it, forming an upside-down horseshoe shape. I love that sacrifice face! Generally a stoop-shouldered—better stop here so as not to encourage wrong sort *turismo*.

    Bests,
      El Presidente
      Bélà Lugösi.

▪ 12 ▪

Impossible get those leaves to NYC in time to be effective baby boom stoppage. Also what dosage. We're working on it, even so, packaging is the hang-up. It's all yellow with cougar urine stains, and there are brown spots on the dosage instructions, on crucial words—*A.M.* and *ballyhoo* and *orifice*. Must repeat MUST trace 'em to Amazon source up jungle or else breeder normals'll flounder in morass of mini-

Hot Dog ends up Hot Girl.

▪ 13 ▪
PARIS PISSOIR.
Zouave: "Why are you carrying so many loaves?"
Mustachio Gent: "Er—I live in the country—"
Zouave: "Feed this—non-organic—"

▪ 14 ▪
Crazier mix here. Spooning by the ocean, barricaded against the African Experience. Ill-fitting composites: hot pants, cloches, pink curlers hanging from plastic sandwich wedges on charm bracelets. Lady in evening dress. Hot movie kiss, pelvic thrusts against escort. Her vw takes off. With a happy sigh, on the outside looking out, aware he must hammer at the outer edge of the outermost shell of a new exterior phase, The Gringo, wearing an immaculate white shirt, finished his last joint, swallowed his last mild pep pill and crossed the frontier.

▪ 15 ▪
At the stroke of six, the lost panorama struck up its song.

Zone B   another in Zone H   Zone B
virile life   mad colonel   virile life
no facilities   cycle   no facilities
                 natural zonings
                 ABCDE
                 cicadas
                 ABCDE
                 natural zonings
bobbing   a leaf-cutter ant   bobbing
dismantle   Futbol Nite Club   dismantle
Zone X   another in Zone W   Zone X

falling feathers   red   falling feathers
no operas   glutted mongrel   no operas
abolish W   Nazi bare patch   abolish W
                 watch out you
                 watch out you
                 cicadas
                 watch out you
                 watch out you
lit up birds   circling over   meat markets
wing edge   no FBI no FBI   wing edges
cut off Amazon   mezzo   in mid-cad

puma-eyed guys   lean out windows   Sundays
humming songs   of lives   lived real heavy
grass rustles   from ungainly   cranings of
            beaks and masks
            beaks and masks
                milky
            trees and vines
            trees and vines
grass rustles   from ungainly   cranings of
humming songs   of lives   lived real heavy
puma-eyed guys   lean out windows   Sundays

sanitary gobbet   sun   sanitary gobbet
wing edge: saw   sun   saw: wing edge
rubber bra   firecracker   rubber bra
                death candy
                death candy
                    do it
                death candy
                death candy
giant awakes   nodding off   giant awakes
men shovel   the nuts will buy   putt-putts
baby girders   nodding off   baby girders

```
some sort      gov't loudspeaker      answer here
bad  gas       not firecracker yet         bad gas
some sort      gov't loudspeaker      answer here
               watch out you two
               do it          do it
                   watch out
               do it          do it
               watch out you two
change subject                        change subject
humming bird                          humming bird
out  of  reach           feast        out  of  reach




let's fuck he said              he said let's fuck
Mawarye and Woxha          Woxha and Mawarye
me too he said       we fuck       he said me too
               watch out you two
               do it          do it
                   watch out
               do it          do it
               watch out you two
the honeyfish        inside her        bit off a cock
lost your cock                         lost your cock
I  know          Woxha  weeps            I  know
```

she told us not to   she told us not to
picked up   taru seed   picked up
picked up Mawarye   Mawarye picked up
           push in   push in
        make new make new
            just fine
        make new make new
           push in   push in
let's fuck he said   he said let's fuck
Mawarye and Woxha   Woxha and Mawarye

overcast again   "Ada"   again overcast
departure today   today departure
live for a moment   and   light up a Torre
             lentils
             feast
             feast
             lentils
white heron   stared at   pleasure boat
one Paris one NYC one Belèm one Chicago
one São Paulo   one Zurich   one El Capitan
      sloth on tree   sloth on tree
         fish leap
           rum
           sun
           ate

Song Lyrics I

Lie With Me, Sweet John

from MISS JULIE

CHRISTINE

Wind around me like Satan's snake, Sweet John.
Swallow the midsummer sun,
Or the welcome shadows will never come,
And where in the sunlit night can we find a haven?
Lie with me, Sweet John,
And make the rivers flow faster.

Circle around me like a giant hawk, Sweet John.
Cover the stars with moss,
And bury the moon in a mound of grass,
And when the sky is as black as the wing of a raven,
Lie with me, Sweet John,
And make the mountain snow melt.

Hop on my hand like a lucky toad, Sweet John.
I'll build you a nest of leaves,
And fondle and feed you as long as I live,
And hold you to my heart when they fill my grave in.
Lie with me, Sweet John,
And flowers will bloom all winter.

They

They walk with a radio clutched to one ear
When they go to the park for some sun.
They have hair like a brand-new experimental product
That comes two for the price of one.
  They have eyes the color of blubber
  And skin like warm foam rubber.
    They.
They are known as *They*.

They stand by a movie house, stare at the line.
Tell me, who's ever seen them go in?
They don't eat, *They* don't drink, but *They* swallow tiny pellets.
They get nourishment through their skin.
  To look more like one of the masses,
  At night, *They* wear dark glasses.
    They.
They are known as *They*.

  When you answer a telephone, "Hello. Hello . . ."
  And there's only a click,
  It's one of them getting to know you better,
  And not a trick.

They stand near a stock market, pass IOUs
Back and forth, back and forth, back and forth,
And their winter is like spring is like summer is like autumn.
Going south is like going north.
  When *They* cry, *They* cry very clear drops
  Of plastic, not real teardrops.
  Everybody knows they can't be real.
  Oh. Another thing. *They* can't feel.

They marry a mannequin dressed in a mink
That *They*'ve stolen at night from a store.
With a flick of their wrist, their mate is animated,
And *They* always go back for more.
    They don't know the meaning of worry.
    They never sweat—or hurry.
            They.
    They are known as *They*.

They go to the city dump, pick out some parts
By a process *They*'ve yet to reveal.
And *They* add some ingredients. Whoopee! It's a baby!
With a nervous system of steel.
    Plus a lifetime guarantee: Dirt proof.
    Also Love proof. Heart proof. Hurt proof.
            They
    Soon are known as *They*.

    With phony fingerprints on their gloves,
        "Who's there? Who's there?"
    They remove one of us.
    The coroner writes down NATURAL CAUSES.
    Why make a fuss?

In daytime, their headlights are always turned on
In case *They* meet a funeral parade.
With their lips tightly shut, *They* can duplicate real laughter.
When *They* smile, children grow afraid.
    They prefer anonymous faces.
    And anonymous places.
    And hundreds spring up every day
        Of that curious species
        Of neutral He-Shes
            Known as
            They. *They*.
                They.

Brazil

Why are Big Fæces
All taking big DCs
That fly to the land of Brazil?
Where Mafia mobsters
Are gorging on lobsters
And pet parakeets sweetly trill:

No extradition!
Nya Nya Nya Nya Nya
Nya Nya Nya Nya Nya
No extradition!
Nya Nya Nya Nya Nya
Nya Nya Nya Nya Nya

That's why Big Fæces
Are taking big DCs
That fly to the land of Brazil.

Insider traders
And corporate raiders
Love clipping coupons in Brazil.
And butch CIA men
Who once entrapped gay men
Wear ermine in case of a ch–ch–ch–ch–chill.

As catching malaria
Couldn't be scarier,
Presidente Cleenton won't invade Brazil.

Ex-Whitewater grifters
Lift Armagnac snifters,
Live high off the hawg in Brazil.
Hillary in the shadows
Sings Portuguese fados
With dames who can dance like a drill.

No extradition!
Nya Nya Nya Nya Nya
Nya Nya Nya Nya Nya
No extradition!
Nya Nya Nya Nya Nya
Nya Nya Nya Nya Nya

When gains are ill-gotten,
There's only one spot in
The whole world to aim for—Brazil!

In Rio Janeiro,
I'll live like a pharoah.
Whenever I'm hot for a thrill,
I'll fling pearls and rubies
At girls with big boobies
If they say, "Si si si, I w-w-w-w-w-w-will!"

I guess I won't wanna fish
Cause of piranha fish,
So I'll go catch a toucan
Where even Canadian Mounties can't get their man!
Brazil! Brazil!

No extradition!
Nya Nya Nya Nya Nya
Nya Nya Nya Nya Nya
No extradition!
Nya Nya Nya Nya Nya
Nya Nya Nya Nya Nya

One Night Stand

There are two extremes of love.
One extreme is "legit."
The ring bit. The groom bit. The bride bit.
Which leads to the Lord-only-knows-how-I-tried bit.

The other starts with a casual come-on,
And ends with a casual split.
But being an amorous tidbit
Can lead to the Why-did-I-do-what-I-did bit.

Nut-brown eyes. Silky black lashes.
Cups his hand. Tap Tap go his ashes.
Tends to use
The verb *enthuse.*
One Night Stand.
Keep it a One Night Stand.

Nibbly ears. Kisses like fire.
Profile nice. But big rubber tire.
Jokes are stale.
Gets high on ale.
Mister Bland.
Keep it a One Night Stand.

He looked so clean-cut,
He made me feel raunchy.
Now it's End of Scene. Cut.
How'd he get so paunchy?

Skips the news. Flicks through the funnies.
Chews his food like twenty Bugs Bunnies.
        Rasping cough.
        Go knock it off!
        Not my brand.
    Keep it a One Night Stand.

        When I first spied him,
        Loved every freckle.
        Now I can't abide him.
        Bring back Dr. Jeckyll.

Boyish smile. Yes, you're endowed, dear.
Undershorts and voice are too loud, dear.
        Nervous tic.
        A taxi, quick!
        Bye, little brother.
    Aren't you glad you had another
One—   Have fun!
Night—   Don't let the bedbugs bite!

        One
            Night
                Stand!

Marry With Me

from THE GRASS HARP

CATHERINE CREEK
I wonder if he was the Bill
Who had a tattoo on his chest—
A hussy all undressed.
He was a plumber.
Came to fix my faucet.
Didn't have the tools to find the leak.
He lasted out the week
And stayed the summer.
Played the ukulele.
Miss him daily
When I hear a drip.

Yeah! He's the Bill who wrote: Marry with me,
Won'tcha   Marry with me,
Catherine, Marry with me.
Marry with me, Love, Bill.

Or was he that sweet-talkin' Bill
Who peddled his line door-to-door.
The local agent for
The Book of Knowledge.
Paid the first installment.
Volume One, which went from A to C,
He read out-loud to me.
Just like a college!
Got up to Columbus.
He took some bus.
Still off on that trip.

Yeah! He's the Bill who wrote: Marry with me,
Won'tcha   Marry with me,
Catherine, Marry with me,
Marry with me, Love Bill.

Could have been the Bill who built my chicken-coop.
Took off on his own on a Pullman job.
Could have been the Bill who liked my chicken soup.
       Uh-uh, no. His name was Bob.

          Bill,
    The heftiest man on the scene,
       He kept my garden green.
       Did all my seedin'.
       Muscles looked so ripply!
   Didn't dare refuse him what he ast,
       The high point of my past—
       What I been needin'.
       Lasted up to autumn.
       Could have caught him
       If I'd had a whip.

Yeah! He's the Bill who wrote: Marry with me,
    Won'tcha   Marry with me,
    Catherine, Marry with me.
       Marry with me, Love, Bill.

       Known a peck of Bills.
       How could I tie the knot?
   The only letter in all my life I got
      Said: Marry with me.
    Won'tcha   Marry with me.
    Catherine, Marry with me.
       Love, Bill.

Who'll Prop Me Up in the Rain
from CITY JUNKET

Z

Jumping Judas, it gets my goat,
I pay taxes. I vote.
I walk when the flashing signs say WALK
I don't jaywalk.
I signal when making a right turn.
So it's my turn. *My* turn.

Hey, I'm patriotic!

I choke up when bugles play Reveille!
And when I hear Taps, I breathe heavily.
Sympathy? Hah! No one thinks my blues real.
I feel like a zeppelin I once saw in a newsreel.
One second, okeydoke.
Then whoosh! It's up in smoke.

No comprehendez the lingo.
Why is *my* hair turning gray?
I never get to shout Bingo.
Bring back the U.S. of A.
Bring back the U.S. of A.

No exit. No can skedaddle.
Everything's going kerflooey.
I'm up shit creek with no paddle.
Even the air-conditioned air smells pee-yooey.

A loser. No pot to piss in.
Nothing of value to pawn.
Aw, who has the patience to listen?
All gone. All gone.

Used to be
When it poured down cats and dawgs,
I'd go prop up apple branches, and talk purty to the hawgs.
    Laughing at the thunder,
    Watching lightning streak,
    Naked as a jaybird,
    I'd plunge into the creek.
    What I want to know is:
    When my high times wane,
        Who'll prop me up in the rain?

    Used to be
I'd find skulls with giant jaws.
I'd find porcypines of bone, and old turkey buzzard claws.
    Prowling in the backwoods,
    Through a dark ravine,
    Naked as a jaybird,
    Back when I was green.
    What I want to know is:
    When I'm dead and gone,
        Who'll prop me up in the dawn?

Some bumbling bird,
Who'll pick me up,
Turn me round, peck a bit,
Stare a while and start to smile
    At my remains.

What I want to know is:
When my high times wane,
    Who'll prop me up in the rain?

All I want to know is:
When the good times end,
    Who'll say, come on in, my friend.

Andrei's Lament

from THREE SISTERS

ANDREI

This town is two hundred years old, Sophia.
Population: one hundred thousand, Sophia.
One hundred thousand people
Who look alike, think alike, talk alike.

This town has yet to produce
One artist, one philosopher,
One scientist, one saint—
One individual of any distinction.

Its one hundred thousand inhabitants
Eat, drink, copulate, sleep, and die,
Producing perfect replicas who
Eat, drink, copulate, sleep, and die.

To lend spice to their humdrum lives,
They indulge in dreary little vices:
    Cards and vodka,
    Malicious gossip,
    Petty thievery.

The husbands cheat on their wives.
The wives cheat on their husbands.
They pretend to be fine, upstanding folk,
And the weight of their hypocritical lies

Crushes the life out of their offspring,
Who soon become deaf-and-dumb sleepwalkers,
Marooned in a city of the dead,
    Like their ancestors,
    And *their* ancestors,
    Going back two hundred years.

I used to enjoy life, Sophia.
I was clever, amusing—good company.
My thoughts and dreams were full of variety.
The future still "beckoned."

Now I know what life is all about,
I've turned into a deadly bore,
A pompous ass whose life consists of
Overcooked goose and greasy cabbage,
And flatulant after-dinner naps.

    Ah, yes. And sponging off other people.
    Other people exactly like me, Sophia,
    Other people exactly like me.

Beauty Secrets

from LOLA

LOLA MONTEZ
Naked in the night, a handsome devil of a lad.
Naked in the dawn, a self-appointed Galahad.
Babbling on and on
How I'm his Great Love, His One Love.
I hate love! I hate love! I've done Love.

All the same,
After we've kissed, kissed and kissed,
Don't let him crinkle up his nose
At the wrinkles round my wrist.

Beauty Secrets,
Promise not to fail me.
Don't let him see me as I am,
In the cold hard light of day.

Beauty Secrets,
If you have to, veil me,
To distract him from the fine points
Of my disarray.

If I'm asleep, and he's awake,
Don't let him stare
At a strand of hair,
Wriggling down my neck,
Flecked with gray,
Giving me away.

When we're lying, naked in the dawn—
If midnight doubts assail me,
Promise you won't fail me,
Beauty Secrets.

Moving Right Along

Easter Poem for Joe '79

Your real Easter poem may be a little late this year,
due to my knack for sitting
in the recurrent starlessness
speed forgetting.

Jane Fonda, so soon.
Meltdowns, daffs in prissy clumps
growing out of hallowed Loew's Sheridan soil.
I'm a mixed-layer micro-organism myself,
skating over the imbedded conning tower,
prone to clayey metamorpho—
have media habit bad.
Variety grosses, the personals,
the new chains, reviews of chains,
phlegm, phlegm. Shelled the peas.
Flubbed *Golgotha* in the puzzle today.

Skipping fear-and-loathing eons,
trim bodies are back in the side streets.
Saw a housefly between Venetian blind slats,
sitting there saying howdy its way.

Hope to rough all this out by Flag Day,
smooth it down into workable emotional units by Halloween,
laid out like tourist cabins in a border clash by Thanksgiving,
a period piece that refuses to shut down by New Year's,
with sediments too balky to settle by—Easter.

Dead ends, fresh starts.

Moving right along.

Squatter in the Foreground
—for Ann Lauterbach

We rake the past, down to an ounce of wants.
Meant to begin in haybarn dorm of overall kerchiefs,
an empire of cow sphincters on the hook by May.
I think I'll stare at the muss to endure
all I am: nonstop strands, new dues to pay up.

Air dense with leavings, fridge hum clicks off.
Nothing on the easel, so nothing melts.
The story thus far: pair of angels swish across grass
into dim room. Wrestlers. Big mirrors, stacks of 'em.
White walls lift. An Anglo-Saxon pause for identification.

Black Froth

Lugged in the green tomatoes, late as usual.
Busy summer emplacing concrete X's
in the variegated fortress boxes.
Press foot, release, flush them down,
miniaturized, into a new trajectory,
burrowing through vast distances
high above the firestorms
flashing around us unseen and unheard
as we go about our daily chores:
squash to be grated *con amore*,
pickerel to be scraped clean of primal filth,
coin on fish-eye the custom up here,
sacerdotal interlude among the falling leaves.

Parsley remains to be snipped and bagged,
tagged for the season of retrenchment ahead.
More laggard than usual, so basil blasted,
remnants bitter to tongue.
Woke up, panting hot hound pace
from appointed rounds: thrusting
penis into marsupial pouch,
abdominal region of accomodating freak.

Authorities assert speed-up techniques
set our bio-clock hands whirling so fast
they form crimson blur-of-blood circles—
bull bait and we're bull,
ritual to keep America America,
watching the past form into sample dynasties
forking out with room to spare,
the paramecium and amœba chalk talk
of our mountain peak childhood above tree level.

Intended to be object lesson
to get out with it
while gun, gung-ho—
but a numbing starts,
as if jungle leaf ingested,
pleasure jaunt,
seat belt silenced, motor coughs its last,
coasting into godforsaken rest area,
corrugated picnic tables untarnished.
Infantile fecal gougings and regurgitations,
macerations and flood-cosmos-with-urine—
outer limits of this lotus status.
Rescuers on the way!
Sandstone god hulks babble curses,
merely a zephyr moseying up the valley of boulders.

The few protected stalks under glass are oblivious
to the rapid-fire alterations going on around them,
as I am, in my way, harping as is my wont
on the old-style voyages with the perquisites spelled out,
the amenities underlined thrice.
One factual detail I can vouch for:
weekends were set apart for roadhouse adventures
at the dirt trail junctions where sidewalks ended.
The ditty on the jukebox would climax, brass,
jitterbuggers a-whirl. They'd part,
start back to booth,
but what with the mirrored pillars,
glimpse of self as stranger,
state of terror,
it'd start up again.
Back to the floor.

Later on in life,
Stranger shadow self
ends up under the bedclothes,
panting as you wake up,
fucking the freak.

Disjointed a necessary mode of life ill-prepared for.
Eager for the seamlessness underneath
caught in the flashlight beam
down in the caves the excursion mobs aren't shown.
Explained all this to the napping man in the booth,
toll booth. Just plaster and paint effigy
to discourage abberant something-or-other.
Traffic backed up to the white foothills aglow in the dusk.
Lots of time and foodstuffs to settle in
to this fabled paradise of glittery adornment,
each particle of the omnipresent nakedness unique.
No word for it in our dialect.

Which leaves the five-day periods, Monday thru Friday.
Clean underwear. Keep out of sun's way.
Lie low when the moon turns "amusement park"
up there among the outposts called black holes nowadays,
when we remember to,
bringing in the onions, nights,
tardy as always.

Monster Worship I

Where Nureyev was rolling in the red fjord in the red Ford with Robert Redford on our way to Horror Wood, want it? Squeezeplay, till self-eject into mackerel sky, bounce like rare Hadrian and continuous loins playing leapfrog in the sky, each territorial whoozis they land on marks dawn of a New Bwana. Meanwhile, we slog through a Magic Knot line of our own devising, weighed down by ten-words-or-less Geezer Girls, voids carried in cement-bag fashion. Boomlet psychology blinds us to the noxious stench of rubbery super-structures, trees scraping against the weather dome: no reentry. Undone by wind.

Monster Worship II

Hair comes out in tufts—sun dance,
finger dance of Wannabe Lake entre-
chats projected up on a bedsheet. Red
ropes close off Old Folks hum—half-
eaten clam dip-and-Brie soufflé (fang
marks), hair-net on a cocoanut shell,
crazies making like on a fruit binge.
Wringers squeeze arms out to proper
highway length sea-to-sea, the young
hopping up and down clawing at the
screens squeak-squeak-squeak. Front
porch o'ergrown with trumpet vines
sandwiched between Moon-Z towers.

Communications Equipment

Fall output hotbed.
Sorted out algebraic mosaic
buckles from skywave, wrap it up!
Sun up in sky frontal straight
veers off into coyote yowl
issuing forth from human throat.
Go-between wizardry, thrill of.

Over to picaresque puttering,
cut off from channel of dubbed-in choice.
Cut-off point is what I do,
down to amuse through trapdoor,
flea circus in muffin (interior buzz)
to which add chortles at the portholes,
glutted bubble-dancers glaring out,
lip-read answers wearing thin,
folderol about mutt bumblebees
zonked on cold mums,
bone orchard mums cat's night out.

Kinky gentry into ransom crud used up.
Holding our own in flustery weather used up.
Many restful oases here in Hat City,
same old snappy salutes at the roadblocks
where om-like hum of shoot-out traffic
of scant interest to us fine-eared hold-outs,
honed to love outcries in the painted desert,
shrieks from humanoid wind tunnels.

Youth blur memory descends the staircase
now hidden by rock formations
and out the door.

Undervalue love object, fear of death rattle.
Overvalue love object, fear of breath battle.

Strobe allows scant time to dredge deep—
microscopic attention span units
run for cover like clobbered roadrunners
seeing bio-feedback chameleons in the sky,
hammers and fireworks pulsating,
tickertape huzzahs.

Hula biz for rent,
mood music booed.
What first President underwater reef,
riding in an auto to Mobile offshore.

Moth-eaten defeats bombard the senses.
Totaled hotbox.
Who said hot wax?

Tiptoe through the hydrants
out to where orange dabs
(shy dance) carouse down
like silly symphony moths,
strident franchises
of dried A to Z embryos.

Here comes the goof
Looking for proof,
he of the baffling accident pile-up,
airline an almost not there line,
bolero about defective sky forests,
leafless but rare.
We never close,
radio low,
flash flood.

August

Now coming up on scherzo,
simulated situation based on big, big trouble.
Word good as broken-down bond,
suspicious circumstances veer off
into thruway marauders with wooden gourds,
virgin tots and oldsters offered up for sugar cubes,

Stubble got on underdog statuary,
stubble, half-eaten steel-plated tuna-on-rye,
stubble, dandruff on cowlick,
stubble epileptic shot-glasses on shelves,
stubble cancer spansules
floating down on the electorate
trucked in from Bosnia.

Module of fezzes and loincloths unscathed.
Weird to peer under shrubs in his likeness.
Based on actual wars, that park,
real-life guns and kitchen implements
pointing at old man ankle-skin and hair.
They left office so fast!
Food drops in the mine warrens resumed.
Pine barrens cordoned off, resumed.

Now coming up on the obligatory slow movement.
Have a protracted adolescence, you dudes,
wandering through dark misty barns,
feisty bites on the kisser,
tracing trolley tracks through the rain forest.

One poignant moment worth a recap:
fœtus sees giant foot.
Giant foot sees giant centipede.
Then the technicalities take over,
pushing us to the sidelines.

Malpractice vivisections
ooze to the lab tiles,
squalid ephemera tallied,
esoterica rendering years in white smocks
invalid, in mountains where no birds fly.

Not my years!
Ablaze with loops of light,
like a dream factory in a ballet at top speed,
candy factory corridors under the slagheap, sped,
factories where steam wisps whisper niceties
about four-wheel mentalities.

Now coming up on coda wobble,
revenge against so much glare
grinding to a stop
in a servantless world.

In The Sky

Nova we call them now.
Mangled envelope arrives, doodled on.
Hope to overleap this safe-from-attack era of nocturnal splurges.
Bottles rattle in the medicine cabinet in the traumatic wee hours.
Good discipline to compete with globular clusters.
Been over all this raw material for quite some time.
Tentative feelers prod for soft underbelly.
Archives of rehashes are bursting at the seams.
Crops on roofs?
Deep nap on raft in a colonial setting.
Gardens moving past at hectic pace.
Sometimes fancy Socratic rhetoric breezing through the stars,
The rejoinders caught up with by the vehicles
Deliberately scrambled by Gawd jawing.
Charred gloop upgraded into cloud formations
Of a grotto for an audience of one.
The heritage part is getting hazier by the second
Due to rapacious souvenir hunters after the splintered bits.
But much advancement into expanded spaces as yet disease-free.
Up to us
To link up disparate inner workings of you and me.
Accentuate if-you-can-step-in-it-you-can-eat-it dialectic.
Eliminate let-me-sew-you-to-your-sheet syndrome.
Deadly cul-de-sacs. Atop hills.
A spoof of food and blood echo.
Obesity ramps slicked up.
Down into the bowels of the Power Sta.
The seam between crazy past and sane present,
Animal and—whoa there!
Hold it! Second wife coming through clear now.
Telegraph offices thing of past.
Second wife society nitwit.

Third wife kin. Fourth height.
Five, pneu. Six, well-boiled icicle.
Seven, heaven. Stop! Stop right here, and good luck!
Tight security. Chain fences around the potato fields.
Glaze coating the heavens with blue glaze,
Adulterated to eliminate glare factor.
Sage replies lost art.
Bill hard at work on a fetid board in distant cities.
His crow, Spondulicks, pecked at the Halloween leftovers.

One Hundred I Remembers
Inspired by Joe Brainard

I Remember wearing glasses for the first time. Leaves and branches looked amazingly clear.

I Remember vomiting (to my horror) on Shirley Temple's framed photograph, which I kept on my bedside table as I was sure I'd marry her when I grew up, partly because we were both born in April.

I Remember knitting a scarf (Navy Blue) for Bundles for Britain World War II which when it finally reached a decent length, was so ratty-looking, I ended up hiding it in a closet.

I Remember telling a lady in a diner on a train that I was a British War Orphan, and how my family'd been killed in the Blitz, except for Aunt Gladys, who went insane from the shock.

I Remember continuous dreams I could keep going from one night to the next.

I Remember time machine fantasies, of returning to the past, generally Elizabethan England with modern inventions such as cars and beauty parlors, and being hailed as a hero.

I Remember saying "Thank you, Ma'am" whenever we went over a little hill in the car, if the resulting bump made a ticklish sensation in one's stomach.

I Remember swinging at the top of Ferris wheels when new passengers got on and old ones got off.

I Remember X-ray machines in shoe stores in which one could see one's foot bones.

I Remember losing a tooth in a salad.

I Remember being a slow eater.

I Remember being told to finish every morsel on my plate because of the starving Armenians.

I Remember sitting at Starvation Corner—last to be served.

I Remember bending down, and touching my dick with my own tongue, fully aware one day this wouldn't be possible.

I Remember tennis games and sending up prayers to God so I'd win.

I Remember giving up believing in God, and wondering if I'd be struck by lightning as a result.

I Remember being called Nicotine Fiend at boarding school because a carton of Chesterfields was found in my bureau —against the rules.

I Remember helping set a house on fire because it was "haunted"—i.e. empty. The Headmaster told us it was our duty as Christian gentlemen to come forward and confess. No one did.

I Remember sending away for stamps "on approval" and then just keeping them.

I Remember drawing evening dresses for women, with plunging V necklines. I couldn't draw hands so I hid them behind the dress.

I Remember hearing a cabdriver say "Cocksucker" and figuring out what it meant.

I Remember a hernia operation, being given gas. An endless tunnel vibrated with a buzzy nightmare sound, a tunnel into which I fell, faster and faster.

I Remember the problem of hard-ons in short pants, and, once, being photographed with one. There it was, for all to see, but no one seemed to notice it.

I Remember going through wartime trains, coach after coach, staring at sleeping sailors, and the bump on one side of their white pants.

I Remember getting a crush on a particular soldier on a train, a Lon McAllister look-alike, and sticking a wad of chewing gum under my Pullman seat—a wad that somehow ended up on the handle of his knapsack under the seat.

I Remember walking around with my fly unzipped.

I Remember a man in Grand Central Station asking me to come to his hotel room. He showed me a photo of his wife and kids. I said no. I looked down. My fly was unzipped.

I Remember listening to soap operas ("Ma Perkins") on the radio when I had whooping cough.

I Remember planes spiraling down into the ocean (learners) at Coronado Beach, California, during World War II.

I Remember asking for wire coat-hangers, door-to-door: scrap metal.

I Remember water mirages, in summer, on streets.

I Remember meeting an albino baby.

I Remember never being able to see Pikes Peak, which was part of a wall-like mountain range that rose in the distance beyond the house—The Rockies.

I Remember tourist cabins. My father owned some.

I Remember prairie dogs, sitting up in front of mounds, little paws hanging down.

I Remember tumbleweed speeding across the prairie.

I Remember seeing an electric automobile driven by an old woman who wore a black silk ribbon around her neck.

I Remember playing Parcheesi. And Mah Jong.

I Remember the smell of a croup kettle, my favorite smell of all.

I Remember how my sister Vivien and I sent a genuine Swiss governess back to Switzerland by cracking our knuckles at the dinner table at a prearranged signal, and then running around like crazy.

I Remember Miss Peters—another governess—not a genuine one, who drank cokes with every meal, including breakfast.

I Remember listening to Gilbert and Sullivan and Wagner on records that had to be stacked inside the Magnavox.

I Remember the family gathering in the library to listen to Hitler rant on the radio.

I Remember going downtown with my father to the Ute Theatre and asking if the urinal with water that gushed at intervals was an Indian invention.

I Remember my father broke an egg into a top hat at my birthday party, and (magic trick) it didn't make a mess.

I Remember my favorite set of stamps: different pastels, black border, Belgian, in memory of Queen Astrid, who'd died in a motor accident.

I Remember never bothering to learn the words of "America the Beautiful" at Assembly, but I moved my lips anyway.

I Remember my father, in the middle of the night, waking me up to tell me my mother had died. The last thing she told him, so he said, was *Be Kind.* For a long time this stuck in my mind, as if it were an admonition of gigantic importance that applied to me too.

I Remember before the funeral kissing my mother good-bye on the lips. They were cold and frightening.

I Remember believing, at that age, that I could predict Death, because I'd had a hunch she'd die. And because I'd had a hunch a pet dachshund, Belinda, would die, and she did.

I Remember believing if I thought hard enough of my mother, she'd come to life in the sky place where she'd gone.

I Remember seeing a rattlesnake.

I Remember shuffling through the garden in winter, in galoshes, imagining I was being pursued by Nazis in Czechoslovakia.

I Remember German-Jewish refugees.

I Remember how horses bored me.

I Remember how duck hunting at dawn with my father bored me.

I Remember how I practiced tennis, solo, against a backboard—hour after hour—without being bored.

I Remember eating raw peas out of the vegetable garden.

I Remember the first cherries in summer.

I Remember homemade ice cream.

I Remember wooden ice-boxes.

I Remember drinking "beef juice" to build me up.

I Remember watching Diana Thurber pee, in a stable, and holding my hand under her so it'd get wet. Someone interrupted us.

I Remember being taken to see a famous movie star who lived not far away from us in Colorado. Her name was Gilda Gray and she was famous for inventing The Shimmy.

I Remember meeting the Abbeys, a famous family who'd gone around the world and had written a best-seller about their travels. The main thing that interested me was that they'd bathed nude in Russia.

I Remember three-day (?) train trips from Colorado Springs to NYC, and changing trains in Chicago.

I Remember the main advantage of lower berths—staring out at night at small-town stations.

I Remember the way trains one passed slowly would sometimes seem to be going forward, then backward.

I Remember putting pink squeezy wads in my ears, in NYC, because of the strange sound of traffic.

I Remember thinking, vaguely, kissing led to babies.

I Remember rumors about candy bars that had human fingers in them, because of people falling in the vats of caramel goo.

I Remember seeing FDR—whistle-stop campaign.

I Remember hearing about Bump Days. Bump Days were organized by Eleanor Roosevelt, so that every Thursday, maids' day off, Negro maids would deliberately bump into white women in downtown department stores.

I Remember the Oz books.

I Remember the Dr. Doolittle books.

I Remember seeing a modern dance recital, my first—Hanya Holm—about steelworkers in a factory, with orange-red torsos.

I Remember reading a boring book about Queen Victoria, because my father promised me a present if I finished it. The present was the book.

I Remember being proud I was an English subject and not an American citizen. I felt superior somehow, unique.

I Remember imitating Bette Davis's walk and cigarette gestures.

I Remember trying to see my sister naked in the bathroom, through the keyhole.

I Remember dressing up in sheets (gown). I used tennis balls for breasts.

I Remember my sister Vivien's bedroom ceiling was festooned with her gigantic match wrapper collection.

I Remember going fishing for trout.

I Remember playing the part of a disease in a school production of "Pandora's Box."

I Remember being a tree that stayed put in another production, because I moved clumsily—bad coordination.

I Remember being afraid of breaking bones, and diving.

I Remember flying dreams.

I Remember being afraid of a mysterious Dream Witch in a tree outside my bedroom window.

I Remember getting "hysterics"—laughing fits.

I Remember drinking bottled Poland water as tap water would leave disgusting shit-yellow-brown stains on teeth.

I Remember smoking corn-silk cigarettes and getting sick.

I Remember shitting, and very tiny gold balls began racing around the blue linoleum bathroom floor. Then suddenly they stopped and vanished. I never saw them again, much to my relief, for there was no "rational explanation" for them.

I Remember hobos by the railroad tracks.

I Remember building a shanty-house big enough to crawl into beside our round swimming pool.

I Remember pushing cars around the courtyard in front of our house. I pretended I was driving. One was a green Packard. Another was a green La Salle.

I Remember hugging the son of Edna, our cook, when it was safe.

I Remember throwing pennies at my father, a tantrum, and being sent to a camp for "problem children."

I Remember the attic.

I Remember piano rolls and piano keys going up and down without anyone touching them.

I Remember returning to Colorado Springs when I was twenty-two, and being amazed how small the house I grew up in seemed—compared to my memory of it.

from

Sung Sex

Four Vermont Haikus

▪ 1 ▪
HAROLD BENCHED

Can't hear a thing now.
Phone. Purr. Rattletrap. Sireens.
Same age Virgil T.
Pickup newly fixed. Tempting.
Loves to ride those roads.

▪ 2 ▪
TV LUNCH VT

Steam onion harvest.
Fry garlic in olive oil.
Add smoked ham (small chunks).
Mince coriander. Combine.
Top off with *Young & Restless*.

▪ 3 ▪
SEPT

Backwoods hush. I hear
car doors slam like rifle shots.
Freeze. Sweat. Sudden death.

Cat on a rickety chair.
Hard work keeping white fur white.

▪ 4 ▪
MEDIA MADELEINE

    VCR pulsates
12   12   12   nonstop nonstop
      pee trek 4 AM
flick flashback   fleabag hotel
blind drawn   neon   off on off

Nov 17

—*for Jean Boulte*

River. Sunny day of Hudson River and more river.
Flea market postcards. Halley's Comet exhibit, poet chum visit.
Dusk now. Cul-de-sac: block of river real estate,
depressed. What scares me is history ignored.
The flag hangs in the window long run.
That's all you get. No products inside. Who'd buy?

Fain must round curve, dwell on honey coeks, crullers,
ginger coeks, preserved quinces, broiled shad,
sumptuous autumn pre-effluents, when the ocean
knew its place was downriver. Higgledy vignette.
Surely these days allow one higgledy vignette, tabled,
about no send me Korea, me no furtive sex Commie kook
stuck among applesellers in homburgs: the FBI.
Vamoose, curse of shirtsleeves-to-shirtsleeves!
My demi-urge informant, Red Hoek, has expensive habits—
The River Goddess in the caduceus, replete with human yens
like the underwater woman watching TV underwater,
a chiaroscuro trick: blurry flurry in store window murk.
Out of it. That's all you get. Who'd buy?

Coming ambrosia of river-and-land, a stockpile, as in the soaps,
of amnesia. Beer neon. Cheez-its. Have some Cheez-its.
Chainsaw all you want. Cigarette hack. When I'm bad
I'm better, so don't schmooze your lips on my salty tears.
Phone before digging. Dinner date, so into deep dusk.
Gazebo silhouette. Headlights. Back into thru traffic they veer,
away from solo child playing darts among the regulars.
Random blinks on the far shore the bar's unique round
wooden icebox came from. Lap lap lapping. Blinks. Lap lapping.
Random blinks lapping. Isolation enhancers.

Pullmanette

Look at that beach. Atlantic. Twin liners,
snub-nosed cutouts, white casinos Zambia bound.
Goofy warble. Car alarm. Or ambulance, mini-life support
for Minnie Mouse. Ethnic potage too toxic,
Hispanic Suez. Volatile nostalgia for boohoo ooze.
Parking lot gate slides shut, E-Z electro,
condo eye styling determinism, crowd control smoothie.
Winter warmth so profligate, white-bearded methuselahs
solve conundrums in organic glare. Warble's back.
Asbestos in thrift shop polka dots'll do that—
Minnie's spindly legs knuckle under, spilling cheap fruit.
Takes years for élan to fade in genes dated Praha, pre-*plage*.
Warning. High risk, all you smarmy hand-kissers in golf pants
tethered at the calves. Died in her sleep
watching *Miami Vice*, Classic Coke drained.
We missed wake, mountainous osso buco, marrow gobs,
unregistered subgroup on permanent hold,
cots shoved together for anal sex and crack
where Art Deco gigolos, brilliantined year round,
used to cruise the flying buttress of the old Dutch fort.

Rug Boast

Bizarre as the name he bore—Peru wrapped his guests in rugs to help them adjust to the tilt of the fault. At the up end, the second of my two exposés slid and slid towards The Inspector.

The black speck with the Automatic M-1 kept on shooting at Red City dots on a USA map carpet illuminated by laser beams. Revelatory finale—mourners on a rampage. Coda: snatch jewels out of the display case to doll up The Urn of The Inspector.

A Burn Baby tableau opportunity pinned down the parade of stretch limousines down canyon in the microchip ghetto. The Trade Towers fell sideways—as skedded—on an empty supremacy court ghat. As skedded—that was the twilight I superimposed an ad, a Peru ad, for Mouth Wok squeezed on a tattoo of Burton Rainmaker III, né Renée, née Skeezix *toi*.

In the ocean-going lane, dream sharks nudged Moxie bottles into the Shred Zone: irreparable loss. Self Help phrases like "Timber" were emasculated. Incorrigible density—meretricious thicket of ambiguities deeper down from further back. Clouds of birds turned day into night (suet phase), pecked the cherry off my wife and I's Easter bonnet—bestrewn with cotton candy derricks she mispronounced DEH-WICKS! Oh. Not that this counts as a media non-event—but when we potato-raced each other down the marina, little silk tongues of propane flame—too dark! Visual impact of social satire on fuel nil. That was the day—as skedded—I subbed as a Grad of Math & Bach. Arf-Arf-Arf. Peru stared up Burton Rainmaker III's kilt. Arf-Arf-Arf-Arf. He whispered, "Tall tale gay." Up kilt, it came out "Tattletale Gray" long after the suet phase, though frankly, it didn't terminate right. Suet tapered off irregular, kept coming out nonstop squeezed out into rainbow ribbons. Anyone, uh, with De Luxe stamped on his/her wrists could, uh, just uh, help themselves, uh, to, uh, seconds, uh, and thirds.

A smog of no-knock quark dust dribbled through my head bone. Remarkable. Totally cordoned off, mentally speaking. Curtained inside a booth—me. Good Ol' Boy Spy, watching silhouettes of functionaries bob and scrape. Whadda ritual-ridden tribe. Doze off. Come to. Same frame. No matter. So remarkable, the resemblance of the cloth blotches to Indian pockmarks on the cleft chin. The idol cliff is 12,000 feet high—as skedded. At the down end, the first of my two exposés slid out into the sky, over the Identical Twins—twelve thou strong, circling round a plaza of shadows elongating at dusk.

Kitchen

What with such thick flakes, can't hear myself think. Just stopped. Namby-pamby descent of a few enervated strays as if all eon. Ragtag droop, torn yellow dodging a start up. Memory on fritz. Layabouts on backyard branches no win. Al. Lit match. Gray sole. Squeeze lemon. Wipe dish. Soak pan. Al. Al Zhivago ate a potato. In a drawer, secret potato 4 x 4.

The faucetry demo has 4 4 x 4s. Subtexts. Food Love. It's a Moviola. Sex Love. Paired up like wed. Money Love. Moviola. ?eat? TV gameshow veer, Vanna batwings on rollerskates, humps the pristine blanks. Lingo frottage. Th, tirechain, on wintry country lane, her first diphthong. Th. Th. Th. Death Love, you big lummox! Th. Th. Death Love Moviola 4 x 4.

Plot. Turandot no longer linear, what with sicko flukes, jazz nights, condom machines dotting the palais walkways. Job o'erseas. Feigned Aussie accent in beige pedal-pushers. Talk prices. Feminist ideograms all hers. Gusts from veil dances and flailing sleeves shift 'em 'neath the bushes. Buddha's belly button signifies Death Love, so Moviola drifts past imperial male organ, detumescent, signifying Al. Al Z. Al Zhivago's male individuation is forsworn for *Causa Bella*—a thriller. Now she's eating a winter melon on a rope bridge. Breakfast in the dark, alone. I saw her do it, saw her take off her bra. 4 x 4 Money Love Moviola—hurl lit bra into ebony canyon 4 x 4.

Wrong person (me) in the thriller. Case of mistaken 4 x 4s. Hots swept into the future, last first—my system at its best. Green pyramid upended, trickle down cornucopia, rarities spread about base, yams, pigs already roasted, batteries included for skin tone implants. CIA agents hot to trot. Ah! Al Z 4 x 4s.

Miscalcu . . . supernumeraries press against the vast plate-glass. All 4 x 4 Moviolas at once! Apex lifts off, green pyramid with Man God in it, split from base. Hovers in sky. Rays of white. Cocoon. Stone pediment looks forlorn, shorn of best featurette.

4 x 4 memory. Small towns linked by trams. One day tracks end. Woods. Aha. Lovely mossy dell 'twas. Who knows—gold downriver. Cholera. Chinese? Too tired. No one figures out on hands and knees how to mop up mess. One day, rats ate through the cement and got at the pot. Stoned out of gourds, raced among computers. Al Z is a-straddle the cooler with Turandot. Dots. Miami. Wed. One tepid Junie, nah, Dad and Sis. Rumba bellies ground. Hi Mama, asleep so good in the sky. To my horror, I spied on a fellow in dungarees and he nigh empty the entire contents of the Ketchup bottle (ol' hat joke) on Al Zhivago's 4 x 4 fries. Wafer on water tower. Wolf moon.

Mindless Bliss
—for Ann Lauterbach

A 1942 Kodak, Kodak Moon, was the food of the Gods
way back up in 1943, bobbing along the Rio Iowa.
Abandonéd Ned. 1944 rays: black sweethearts asleep
over and out where cowbirds led us to tuna and copra, 1945.

The Vatican lay blindfolded, 1946, bedded on anthills
dubbed raisins, debtor raisins. Debutante genius, nylon 1947
"Great"—a pabulum of cleavage squinched sidesaddle.
Muffled photo opportunity cast shadows untouched by 1948.

Feds, 1949 infatuation, its thaw
a hype-and-shuck sitcom for redhead sluts and honchos.
Doodlebugs warded off impossible nearness.
Voted concern, 1950, but stay away, dinky birth control dark.

1951 seen from above. Mutt and his tom-toms stood at attention,
all through 1952, alone by the goalpost in the stadium starlight.
Way it works, 1953: sausage factory occupado.
No new zones, not in 1954.

Leaflets dropped Dr. Spock maxims, 1955 ghost president gibberish,
how two intertwined serpents bop on by, 1956 folksy squeeze play.
Another how: how the Great Dwarf Composer, Gilberto, my Pa,
scowled malevolently at the Arctic muck church. 1957. How? How?

Science watch obfuscated by water nymphs in 1958 pouches, that's how.
Body pouches lay deep inside the only g-g-g-girl of 1959,
so it was meat-and-tippy-toe, on the go in 1960 June Land,
UFO mirth, UFO mirth douche, then mirth douche bubbles (bugle toot

USA). Much asylum profiteering. 1961, which led to light year wear,
signed and mumbled 1962. Much as, all asea, Dublin is like Foo King
in traction. Mush push past 1963 detritus via erasure of will.
Ex-informer unbuttoned green gangland, 1964 jungle horror.

Body education steep for war variety.
You know—vittles in perpetuity, 1965, a pantomime for smack, 1966.
Sheep. Beethoven dies unopened. Napoleon conquers Sweden, Pa.
Literary newsreel for our antlered—CENSORED the rest, 1967.

A mogul, plans in embryo, demanded the works. Ah sweet crotch of 1968!
Each shallow dish a labyrinth, its exit 1969, frills like pajama jamborees.
Shithead! Pa. has no Springfield! Just slugger martinets
wintering by a natural lake, spring zenith, 1970 summer haven man-made.

Radio botch. No, it was bitch, a famous huff about an oldie kill fee.
Power lines looped, aloha mode. 1971 autumn, indigent.
Instant fame, due to 1972 codes rigged, famine rules junked.
Fashion models with reggae résumés snorting coke is hunky-dory.

How Maman'd aged! We backtracked around the 1973 moon speedup,
peaceful at last. Airbrushed out 1974 goiter silhouettes,
tenor of hush-hush terrain. 1975 left behind in the breezeway.
Gifts like swatted fish changed hands and pardners.

A bottom line 1976, down the khaki Mississ—
blasé correction. Hot Satiddy ambled under pressed ferns,
a rhythm basic to 1977,
the mad scramble of retreating ice.

Came to 1978, was it? Exposed 1979, continue macramé. Lum's
wobbly psyche more accessible. Answer Balaklava not worth it.
Lure and sleep, sleep and lure. Rammed small gaol in 1980 rock.
Many times! I think much earlier, surmise. 1981 or 1982.

The Thirties
from SUNG SEX

Ideally happy, my first Sung Sex.

That sticky Depression summer of hobos limping along railroad tracks, slum windows were left open, exposed to the elements, no screens, lace curtains long since pawned. Lolling on mattresses plunked helter-skelter on bungalow floors, mattresses littered with Sunday funnies, naked adults fanned themselves, absently, as if in church, Olive Oyl's arms akimbo, jabbing Fritzy Ritz's hairdo, Lord Higginbotham's "Zounds, cad!" momentarily hidden by crotch wadded to lobe squeezed against ankle.

Downtown, luxury apartment buildings, now empty, crammed janitor perverts into basement hovels papered over with Want Ads and scare headlines about blonde chorines found asphyxiated, back-alley mayhem, cement shoes doing the Breadline Shimmy. Tent-show slut knew too much. Saw nothing. Squeal of tires, oozing onto the sawdust, rat-tat-tat-tat.

I wriggled on Dad's lap, my favorite ritual, waiting for green. I heard voices. Herd voices ha ha ha ha ha ha.

VOICES: HE	Wriggled
VOICES: WALKS	Wriggled
VOICES: WITH	
VOICES: ME	Wriggled Wriggled
VOICES: AND	

Yellow turned to green.

VOICES: HE	Lurched forward
VOICES: TALKS	
VOICES: WITH	

Fading away now. Ideally happy. Forgot to mention, voices sang. Sticky stuff ran down my thigh onto Dad's lap.

The Sixties
from SUNG SEX

I'm positive all you graybeard savants, harrumph, recall that
aberrant period when Sung Sex infiltrated the workaday world
of rise-and-shine, transport module, hype spigot, jobjobjobjob
pickmeup, hearth, familial feed, hobby dial, procreation spasm,
death sleep. National holidays? Fantasy ingredients: uplift
myths, inner attainment chores took over, back when leisure
was leisure, work work, and never the twin lobes met.

Some of you Sung Sex Hands out there, all linked up, orifices
scrubbed and scented, scanners in sync, feedback tappers on
the go, some of you Sung Sex Buffs may chortle at government
policies I readily admit I'm in large part responsible for imple-
menting—back in the days when I was Chairperson—we still
had Chairpersons in those dark ages, before transvestite
Chair-tzarinas became all the rage of the SSA—Sung Sex
Authority. We hung in there, the butt of many a joke, let me
tell you—a spinoff of the ARB, Acid Rain Board, to refresh
your memory, which began as an offshoot of the EVP, Environ-
mental Violence Bureau—which evolved out of the original
WCD, Weather Control Department—abolished after the
glacier upsurge scandal. Gosh! I fall behind my story! Shipped
out of Miami in an unmarked garbage dhow, I recall our trés
trés hush-hush transfer to a bathysphere—Haitian registry
—and from there to cramped quarters under a coral reef in the
Caribbean, judging by the marine predators frisking about,
above the ceiling bubble. What a luxury, to be unblindfolded
at last! Ach, I fall so behind. Our dilemma nub—how to arrest
the proliferation of Sung Sex in everyday life: rampant reality
blurrer. We're talking national policy here. Heavy.

Think-tank consensus-wise—the main culprit was the Alarm Clock Radio, pure and simple. Kee-rect! The invention of the Alarm Clock Radio triggered a basic shift in brain upkeep and work ethic enhancement, a shift we suffer from to this day.

To work!
Step A: The Hook up.
Step B: Selected Death Sleepers.
Step C:

LOVE   U   DARL

DARL   LOVE   U

STI   CLOCK   IN   MY   MAU-MAU

TICKN'   AWAY

TH   TH   TH   TH

LOVE   U   DARL

DARL   LOVE   U

LI   TIP   TITTY   MY   MAU-MAU

KWIKEN   DAY

TH   TH   TH   TH

INTERSEXUN

PIP   GOT   PIP

GREEN   LIGHT

POP   HOT   POP

STICKY   POPE

LOVE   U   DARL

DARL   LOVE   U

Switch stations? Same on all. Click it off? Piped in, in the bubble of the coffee percolator, the heart attack-like seizure of the toaster climaxing. Sung Sex echo caroms were set in motion, as he/she/it reached for his/her/its jeans, his/her/its toke, jobjobjob, his/her/its attention span attuned to a new dominatrix, switch it, click it off. No dice. Sung Sex never closed. We Never Closed.

We had it all laid out, the big turnaround. So simple! Work enhancement buzzwords, subliminal infiltration—CLOCK GROUND FLOOR DARL PAYOLA TITTY MOP UP CLEAR OUT TH CEMENT FEET LOVE U DARL RAT-TAT-TAT GREEN LIGHT MINT. They moved too fast out there, the folks. And Moscow had LOVE U KARL beeped in from Siberia while our team diddled. So we lost 'em. One Identity Kit per person? Down the tube. The folks out there were clicking themselves off and on—at will. Their own echo caroms were bouncing around worse than a Demolition Derby in an elephant turd steeplechase—a nation of walking talking human collages. They Never Closed: clicking, shifting, forming intricate personality components, RPM components—Revolutions Per Minute echo caroms intersecting, go ahead, it's green—so Joe Blow could be—at one and the same time—libidinous business Tzarina prowling through the azaleas, Displaced Person sniffing basil on an herb garden bench, not knowing where his/her/its next meal is coming from, flower child rock star, waiting by the cactus at the intersection—embittered by instant fame after a seeming eternity of facelessness.

Even with all our data at their fingertips, the chain of command in hot pursuit couldn't decide what he/she/it should be in hot pursuit of. Alarm Clock Radios at the ready, positioned tellingly—public matters inched, then slid, into a morass—legal, paralegal, no matter. Random turnover became the front burner, meat-and-potatoes bottom line of surv

Special announcement. Our trusty vehicle stalled between grids? What? I've been asked to *what?* Will all you Sung Sex addicts kindly pass your valuables and identity kits to the authorities moving up the transverse in a U formation?

Attention spans built to last a lifetime, sturdy enough to be handed down from one generation to the next, with only minor tinkering, a smiling shark-tooth grille rationale here, a squishy carrot-shaped protuberance taboo there, began to be perceived as part and parcel of a mass hysteria, pie-in-the-sky workaholic cargo cult . . . SPECIAL ANNOUNCEMENT!

> Hear this: Black medallions into the black bus! Blue into the blue, green green. To conserve energy, file out in alphabetical order. If U are impaired, defective physically or psychologically, lie down. A Special Unit'll wheel U to a correct stall.

Skimming Alarm Clock Radio input—angelic, Satanic, love-hate bestiality angst. Must pierce inner ear as atonement. Climax verge, hacked to pieces on the altar. Skimming—bleeding on the bathroom floor, the scent of a wig on fire, waiting for the replacement to arrive, climax, the start of a fresh morning, sound system hooked up.

Dimmer, puh-leez. Tinted Lozenge Kelly: lea-at-dawn jell. Crackerjack. To wind up, all us SSA Operatives began to notice certain dizzying zigzags in the infrastructure. Must leap ahead here. Subgroups content to live in derelict Shermans and under Big Berthas aimed at nothing in particular. Aforementioned subgroups grazed their scrawny goats on the escarpments of downtown intersections no longer in use. On abandoned thruways, squatting, their heads tilted, like hounds under a harvest moon, they listened to a vintage collection behind the chrome window grille of a trivia mart: an Alarm Clock Radio, inadvertently left on, consuming precious juice, dial aglow, permanently jammed into some nostalgia loop or other. Thankee for cooperating, Professor Zbeblewski. *Ciao.*

Lights out. Ancient history. I dropped out.

Song Lyrics II

Schlock 'n' Sleaze R&B
from PALAIS BIMBO LOUNGE SHOW

LAVINIA CLONE
I'm terrible at games,
Always lose at Parcheesi.
Stupid at names.
Saint *Who* of Assisi?

Don't understand Monopoly.
I'm an idiot, I dare say,
And I dress very sloppily.

I think I disapprove of premarital sex.
I wish the world were nuclear free.
To avoid embarrassment when paying checks,
I follow this simple policy.
I go Dutch. Dutch. Dutch.
So how mucho do I owe you for my drinkie, Dr. Moon?
Please let me pay for my drinkie.

DR. MOON
Kinky. Kinky.

LAVINIA CLONE
Your eyes are the eyes
Of a terrifying bug
Invented by Heironymous Bosch—
A tarantula part of me wants to hug,
And the rest of me wants to squash.

If only I knew some magic hocus-pocus
To tenderize the focus
Of your eyes.

DR. MOON
You're Lavinia, babe.
The original mold. You're no Xerox.
Pure Lavinia, babe.
Wanna smother you with rubies and rare rocks.
Lickin' your fangs with your Lavinia tongue,
Caught in a squeeze
Between Schlock 'n' Sleaze.

Wow, Lavinia, babe.
Got a come-hither look like a cobra.
Pow! Lavinia, babe.
Love your black leather scanties and no bra.
A nutso flake, a poco poco too young.
Caught in a squeeze
Between Schlock 'n' Sleaze.

Hang your scuzzy thumb
From your wound of a mouth. Flirty. Flirty.
Whisper X-rated come-ons,
Then get down to it dirty.

LAVINIA CLONE
I want out, Doc.
Spelled O-U-T. Out. Pretty please.
Not my route, Doc.
Sure do miss the birdies and bees.
Pull the lever. Press the button.
Catch you later. Thanks for nuttin'!

Stuck in a crock
Between a rock and a hard place.
Caught in a squeeze
Between Schlock 'n' Sleaze.

LAVINIA CLONE
Lemme go, Doc,
Back home so I can catch some zzzzs.
Yo-ho-ho, Doc.
I'm havin' an I-dentity crise.
I don't need your heebie-jeebies.
Stuff your psychedelic freebies.

Stuck in a crock
Between a rock and a hard place.
Caught in a squeeze
Between Schlock 'n' Sleaze.

Keep climbin' up slimy walls.
Sounds worse than fingernails scratchin' a blackboard.
Deep in my brain, phoney phone-in voices
Yackety-yack. Yackety-yack. Bored?
Terminal ennui
Is closin' in on me.

I want out, Doc.
Spelled O-U-T. Out. Pretty please.
Not my route, Doc.
Hallucinatin' zombies in trees.
Next you'll cram me in a bodybag with seamless seams,
Then gag me so the screams I scream are screamless screams.

Stuck in a crock
Between a rock and a hard place.
Caught in a squeeze
Between Schlock 'n' Sleaze.

LAVINIA CLONE	DR. MOON
I want out, Doc.	You're Lavinia, babe.
Not my route, Doc.	
Lemme go, Doc.	Pure Lavinia, babe.
Yo-ho-ho, Doc.	
s.o.s., Doc	Ooh, Lavinia, babe,
Whisper yes, Doc.	
Lemme go, Doc.	Do Lavinia, babe.
Don't say no, Doc.	

(DR. MOON *holds up the severed head of
Lavinia Sanchez)*

LAVINIA CLONE

Stuck in a crock
Between a rock and a hard place.
Caught in a squeeze . . .

Seventeen Years of Living Hell
from POSTCARDS ON PARADE

VALERIE

Divorces are so messy. Do you mind if we just separate?
As for divvying up the spoils—

> I'll keep the munis, the cyclicals and biotechs.
> The Thirty Year Long U.S. Treasuries.

STAN

> I'll miss your companionship. Sundays full of steamy sex.
> I busted my ass. Tried too hard to please.

VALERIE & STAN

> Threats and spats and floods of tears.
> Trapped in the thrall of an evil spell.
> Seventeen Unbelievable Years of Living Hell.

STAN

> I'll never forget your Gladly, The Cross-eyed Bear.
> Gosh, you were a whiz at charades.

VALERIE

> Remember the time you goosed the derrière
> Of the Dowager Queen of the Philly Kincaids?

STAN

> I'll never forget the look on your face.
> Twenty bucks a point, and I trumped your ace.

VALERIE

On the ballroom floor, you were Twinkletoes!

STAN

I always gave the cha-cha my very best shot.

VALERIE

Hot to trot,
You were quelquechose.

STAN

And you, my prickly honeysuckle rose.

VALERIE

Mouth-to-mouth with that creature! How *could* you!
Whatever became of the chivalrous, good you?

I'll keep the Katzes. The Marisols. The late Matisse.
The Biedermeier bedroom furniture.

STAN

The trips we took. Dropped acid in Greece.
In Athens, mucho flying fur.

VALERIE & STAN

Ghastly smiles and grisly cheers.
Kiss-kiss pretending all is well.
Seventeen Indescribable Years of Living Hell,

VALERIE

Mine, Riviera pied-à-terre.
Yours. Acapulco time-share.

STAN

Mine. The Manet. So exquisite. So rare.
The phoney Monet, yours.

VALERIE

For you, B-girls and barfly whoors.

STAN

For me, CEOs and round-the-world tours.

VALERIE

Mine. The ruby-studded Coptic chalice.

STAN

The good news is: I keep Buckingham Palace!

VALERIE

No more Tiffany vases shattered.

STAN

No more Act Your Age.

VALERIE

No more passion, shredded and tattered.

STAN

No more maniacal rage.

VALERIE & STAN

We've hunkered down so long, alas,
We're a quivering, festering biomass.

VALERIE

Of—Ah-ah-ah-ah-ahngst

STAN

(Correcting her "broad A" pronunciation)

Angst.

VALERIE & STAN
Thanks to
Seventeen years of hysterical screams,
Little white lies and hostility dreams.
Lowdown tricks.
Hit and run.
No quick fix.
Ain't we got fun?

Saved by the bell by the skin of our teeth.
Remind me to send you a funeral wreath.
To celebrate—

VALERIE
How did my charming hippie in sandals
Turn into a bozo with gross love handles?

STAN
You're as declassé as the Queen of Sheba
At a karaoke club, crooning *Ich Liebe.*

VALERIE
Seventeen years of unmitigated—

STAN
Long ago, we should have litigated.

VALERIE
Ten years on the couch, and still a-hankerin' for your Ma.

STAN
You're half Lizzie Borden, and half Blanche du Bois.

VALERIE

Hate to miss the finale of your "How To Go To Pot" Show.

STAN

Love your new image. Wish *I* were that macho.

VALERIE & STAN

Oh, if only we'd never made out!
Fast Forward to Fade Out.
Saved by the bell by the skin of our teeth.
Remind me to send you a funeral wreath
To celebrate
Seventeen Hateful Years Of Living Hell!

Moments in Time

from POSTCARDS ON PARADE

MARSHA II

You in the kitchen. Sweet talk on the phone.
Your shadow looms. The stranger on the beach.
Me in the doorway, listening, spying.
The smell of rain. We share a ripe peach.

Doughboy, my hound dog. Digging for a bone.
Exhibit A. One earring in my purse.
Cannot remember why I was crying.
Jealousy trip. We're under a curse.

Tint it brunette. Makes me look pallid.
Argue all night. Is our love valid?
Climax again. Wolf the egg salad.
       Moments in Time.

Tracing your name on my lips with your thumb.
Joe Babe. Joe Babe. On my lips with your thumb.
All the while crooning some Irish ballad,
       Old as they come.

       Lover sighs.
       Lover dies.
       Couplets in rhyme.
       Moments in Time.

The stranger on the beach.
I must have turned. Did you wave, or—
       Memories to savor.
       So far out of reach.
       Moments in Time.

The earring in my purse.
Like picture postcards to flick through.
Broken bits to pick through.
Some better. Some worse.
        Moments in Time.

Some faded. Some blank.
Don't make a fuss.
You'll scare them off, fragments of us.
Pretty them up. Rearrange them thus.
        Moments in Time.

        Marsha and Joe Babe.
        Moments in Time.
        Joe Babe and Marsha.
        Moments in Time.

Take Me Away, Roy Rogers
from POSTCARDS ON PARADE

STAN

Women. Women
Bite the hand that feeds them.
Who needs them?
I can microwave pizza. I can iron satin bedsheets.
I sound like a nerd
But every word
Is politically correct.
Empower women! Let 'em control all the spreadsheets!
The harder I try, the more I disconnect.
Too gung-ho. Out of whack. Lost my touch.
I don't know whether to reach for the check or go Dutch.

(STAN *unlocks a box, takes out his treasured postcard of Roy
Rogers, and knuckle-wipes a few tears away, unashamedly)*

I've missed your straight-shooter gaze, Roy Rogers,
Tempered by a wary squint.
Though you pre-date technicolor days, Roy Rogers,
Your condition stays mint.
Hear tell your studio went under,
Swallowed, shitty luck, by Sony.
Wonder who's stealing your thunder.
Some androgynous phoney—
Jeans by Calvin Klein.
No friend of mine.

Gee Whiz,
I've lost my fizz.
The Missus gave me the biz.
I'm one trouble-laden trade-in,
Up for grabs As Is.

Since I was a shaver,
And barely could toddle,
You've been my sole role model,
So do me a favor.

Take me away, Roy Rogers.
Take me away.
Where genetically engineered deer and antelope play.
I need therapeutic hugs
From a gang of hairy lugs,
And I don't give a hoot if they're straight as an arrow or gay.

Sure hope they don't smell funny
Doused with nelly eau de cologne.
And what if they call me Honey?
Shoot, I'll ask for a bunk of my own.

Take me away, Roy Rogers.
Take me away.
So I won't be the effigy torched in a feminist fray.
Teach me wilderness survival in a lean-to.
I'm Mr. Nice Guy. But I can be mean too.
We'll share encounter sessions in a tumbledown shack,
With strong silent troglodytes who never blow their stack.

Take me away, Roy Rogers.
Take me away.
Where there are ancient tribal laws only guys can obey.
Too long I've been a wishy-washy Child Man.
Give me a support group. I'll prove I'm a Wild Man!
I'm sick of understudying the role of Dying Swan.
I want to tap into my masculine roots. Star as Iron John.

With a buddy to bunk with.
Powwow with.
Forget the Frau with.
Get drunk as a skunk with.

A prince of a chum to cuss my Ex with.
Arm-wrassle with. Muscle flex with.
A Good 'Ol Boy (thank God!)
I don't ever have to have sex with.

By the old corral,
There'll be wonderful photo ops.
Thanks to you, old pal,
Male Bonding is tops!

Take me away, Roy Rogers,
Take me away.
Giddyap. Saddle up. Yippy-yi-yay.
Giddyap. Saddle up. Yippy-yi-yay.

Soon. Very soon. Maybe some day.
Giddyap. Saddle up. Yippy-yi-yay.

It's A Good Life

from POSTCARDS ON PARADE

STAN
It's a good life.
Bunch of ornery folks
Who put up with dumb jokes.
Mozzarella. Pumpernickel.
Lotsa mayo. Kosher pickle
To go.

THE SIX DEALERS
In rough times, a warm hello.
In spite of cutbacks. Trickledown taste.
Homophobe skinheads. Fanatic control freaks.
Wrapped in the flag. Holier than. Tight-ass security.
One hundred percent straight-laced.

STAN
It's a good life.
Go with the flow. Ups and downs.
Plug-ugly cities. Pretty towns
Where no rooty-tooty snooty varmint sez "Let 'em eat cake."

THE SIX DEALERS
Big Boob Sis. Baby Bro.
Easy come. Easy go.
If you turn round right
So there's plenty of give,
No need to lose zzzzs all het up about The Net.
The Gross. The Take.
And all us chilluns got X-ray eyes that spot: Fake.

STAN
It's a good life.
Not getting any younger.
Ticker still full of hope and hunger.

THE SIX DEALERS

From Jan to December, a member in good standing
Of a crazy off-the-wall kind of voluntary family
That keeps expanding.
Can be demanding.
Depending.
For sure as Buddha made golden apples
There's no such crittur as a Happy Ending.

(Only in stories
Of long-gone glories.)

It's a good life.
Florida tan.
Pick up the van.
Narragansett. Pocatello.
Greasy spoons. Stick to the Jello.

KEVIN
Lookin' great, Stan.

TIM
Dropped some weight, Stan.

SANDY
Give you a special rate, Stan.

THE SIX DEALERS
Motels. Detours. Wall-to-wall malls.
Air unacceptable. Gunk on the beach.
Right on the freeway, bumper-to-bumper, she stalls.

It's a good life.

SANDY
Anybody got a card of a white guy eatin' a watermelon?

THE SIX DEALERS
Happy buyin'.
Happy sellin'.
Happy shoppin'.
Keep on boppin'.

KEVIN & TIM
Lookin' great, Stan.

SANDY
It's a date, Stan.

STAN
Anybody got a card of a white guy eatin' a watermelon on the moon?

SANDY
See ya soon, Stan.

STAN
It's a good life.

Lads

from NIGHT EMERALD

FOUR TOFFS

In every strand, every square
There's a decadent air.
Every toff longs to chafe
For a handsome young waif.

It's the newest of fads—
Gents are loony for lads.
Every rake has an ache
For a tyke on the make.

FOUR RENTERS

Ow's about a light, sir?
Ow's about a smoke?
Pinin' for a mite, sir?
Starvin' for a bloke?

Care to pass the night, sir?
Care to share a pint?
You're a bleedin' s'int, sir.
I'm so famished I could f 'int.

FOUR TOFFS

In every rococo pile
Where there's nary a smile,
Every blade is aflame
For The Love With No Name.

It's the oldest of yens,
Chasing roosters, not hens.
With a chap on your lap,
Joie de vivre's a snap.

TOFF

I gave up my mistresses, my greyhounds and my pipe
For the love of a too-too utterly utter guttersnipe.

FOUR TOFFS

Decrepit duffers with gout
Who once tottered about
Now go waltzing with chums
Commandeered in queer slums.

It's the newest of fads—
Gents are loony for lads.
Ganymede, wearing tweed,
Is seductive indeed.

A tryst with an Adonis is uplifting, if he's pristine.
And resembles Adam on that ceiling in the Sistine.
Chasing classic nymphs is out of fashion—too Philistine!

FOUR RENTERS

Why dally with a floozy, luv?
Buggers *can* be choosy, luv.

FIRST TOFF

Had a nasty shock at dawn.
In flagrante with a faun.
He was a him who was a her.
By Jove! Tricked by a poseur!
Gad Zooks! Or should I say *poseuse?*

FOUR TOFFS

That's what comes of hanky-panky with unmitigated curs!

SECOND TOFF

Some of them try blackmail.
Others steal you blind.
Consorting with these rascals
Does not bring peace of mind.

THIRD TOFF

It's like feasting with a panther.
Strokes you with a velvet paw.
If you ever let your guard down,
He'll unsheath a deadly claw.
Of course, such gross indecency
Is quite against the law.

FOURTH TOFF

If committed with a chum—
Vicious! Vile! Unspeakable!
But I must confess,
In a state of undress
Male torsos are so tweakable.

FIRST & SECOND TOFFS

Aren't they angelic? Angels in a choir.

THIRD & FOURTH TOFFS

Poor innocent dears.
Their rent's in arrears.

FOUR TOFFS

Thank heavens, they're for hire.

FOUR TOFFS

In London Town, every park
Brightens up after dark.
And the smart hoi polloi
Spurn the tart, snatch the boy.

Guardsmen and bootblacks,
Chimneysweeps and drummers.
Grooms and valets
Fan the blaze
Of golden summers.

FOUR RENTERS	FOUR TOFFS
Ow's about a light, sir?	Poshest of trends.
Ow's about a smoke?	Lavender friends.
Pinin' for a mite, sir?	Wing starry-eyed.
Starvin' for a bloke?	Spring to our stride.
Care to pass the night, sir?	Chap on one's lap.
Care to share a pint?	*Joie de vivre*'s a snap.
You're a bleedin s'int, sir.	Newest of fads.
I'm so famished I could f 'int.	Loony for lads.

FOUR RENTERS & FOUR TOFFS
Lads!

Somdomite
from NIGHT EMERALD

BOSIE
Revenge. Sweet.
Hellfire heat
Perfumes me.

Somdomite.
Somdomite
Dooms me.
Dooms me.

I know you disappove of Oscar vastly, Mumsy.
But Papa's done something rather ghastly. Clumsy.
    After many a pint in a pub,
    In Papa popped, at Oscar's club.
    Appalling scrawl on his calling card.
    En garde, Papa. *En garde.*

    Somdomite.
    Somdomite.
Too loutish a brute to spell "Sodomite" right.
You called my beloved a Somdomite,
    And you'll pay, Papa, you'll pay—
    Locked away
    In a dank dark cell
    With a fetid smell.
    And if a guard forces his favors on you—

    Somdomite!
    Somdomite!
What else can I do
But shoot you on sight.

Same dream. Again and again.
Oscar's club. The Albemarle.
Members assembled. Men. Men.
I hear you, Papa. I hear you snarl,
"My son beds down with a Somdomite.
What else can I do, but shoot him on sight."
And Oscar glares with glacial alarm.
Walks off with you, Papa. Arm-in-arm.
   End of dream.

(BOSIE *begins writing a letter*)

How miserable I am, Darling Mumsy.
Father's libeled Oscar Wilde,
And if charges are not brought,
Oscar's name will be defiled.
The Pater we both hate,
He mustn't go scot-free.

I'm in a frightful jam, Mumsy Dearest.
Though the wolf is at the door,
My allowance is all spent.
How am I to launch a war?

We must incarcerate
The monstrous mad Marquis.

Last week, at Monte Carlo, I lost a wad on *Noir*.
My new filly belies her name is *Lucky Star*.

As you know, litigation comes dear.
And Oscar has nary a sou, I fear.
Which brings me to you, I fear.

We must do the right thing. As a family, unite.
Father's branded Oscar Wilde a loathsome Somdomite.

Inventively tribal
But guilty of libel.

Sufficient grounds
To lock him up.
Mumsy, be nice.

Twenty thousand pounds.
To lock him up.
That's a fair price.
Ten might suffice.
Mumsy, be nice.

Smile.
After the trial,
We'll go to a spa.
You and I, *Maman,*
And sup and sup.
And celebrate.

Lock him up.
Lock him up.

As the French say,
Papa's *fou.* Mad.
Baden-Baden.
Marienbad.

You choose.
Sicily. Crete.
A cruise.
No Don'ts. Few Dos.
From *J'accuse*
To *Je m'amuse.*

You've come to my rescue so often.
Oscar and I may part for a while.
Let the set of your luscious lips soften.
        Smile.

        Lock him up.
        Lock him up.

        Future so rosy.
        Bosie and Mumsy.
        Mumsy and Bosie.

        Somdomite.
        Somdomite.

        How I hate him.
        Chains await him.

A Secret Sacred Niche
from NIGHT EMERALD

Paris, 1990. A sidewalk café, late at night. THE DUCHESS OF DEVONSHIRE *has joined* OSCAR, *the final customer, sitting alone.*

OSCAR WILDE

You must call me Sebastian. Sebastian Melmouth is my pseudonym. It would ruin the twentieth century for the English, if they knew Oscar Wilde was still alive, dying beyond his means.

DUCHESS OF DEVONSHIRE
(fishing in her handbag)
Mr. Melmouth, would you honor me by accepting these small *pommes de terre* from the ugliest Duchess in the world? Or have I lost my looks?

OSCAR WILDE

Dear no. You're a late bloomer. You've flowered into the oldest, ugliest, Duchess in all history.
(taking folded bills, summoning WAITER)
Absinthe, *mon petit. Un double.* Duchess? No? Ah, abstention is the secret of ugliness. *Un double,* and the world turns into a garden agleam with night emeralds. After a third and a fourth, I'll hail the first passing perambulator. The end of a perfect alcoholiday.

DUCHESS OF DEVONSHIRE

Sebastian . . . he was the comely saint with the arrows, no?

OSCAR WILDE

Arrows artfully placed. Alas, I have no arrows, just an itch. From a luncheon last spring, of iffy mussels *marinière.* These days, I scratch like an ape. How tactful of you not to feed me a nut.
(WAITER brings him a drink. OSCAR downs it)

Beneath this city of death and disgust,
Where hovering angels see no one to trust,
And sooty skies are black as pitch,
　　　A secret cleft
　　　In a sacred rock
　　Opens onto a quiet niche

Where gods don't pry, and demons don't mock,
Where sweet rain falls on the just and unjust,
　　　And slakes the thirst
　　　Of the blessed and cursed.

Beneath this city of fury and fear
Lies a grotto with water crystal clear.
　　A secret sacred niche.

And there I'll grieve till my heart is content,
And my sorrow and savage rage is spent.
　　A secret sacred niche.

My hollow-eyed double will disappear.
I'll lie cushioned in water crystal clear.
　　A secret sacred niche

Where I'll bid adieu to all earthly delights
And welcome the end of my emerald nights.

Closing time, already? The hotel wallpaper. How I loathe the hotel wallpaper.
One of us has to go. I suppose it may as well be me.

　　　Itch.
　　　Itch.
　　　Itch.

　　A secret sacred niche.

Love Song

from NIGHT EMERALD

—in memoriam Cynthia Weir

BOSIE

Together we defeated ancient dragons of the deep.
We confronted sacred monsters. Away they crept.
Bodies entwined, our sweat mingled as we slept
    When I was young.

All innocence, I entered your paradise, enchanted.
The arrogance of youth! I took it for granted.
How loving you were, at forgiveness, so adept.
    When I was young.
    When I was young.

    Old age longings fester,
    Misremembered in a mist—
Fragments distorted, aborted shapes.
Your voice is drowned by the babble of apes,
    Mocking how we kissed
    When I was young.

You taught me to maneuver
Through the labyrinth of time.
Ensnared by desire, restive in your lair,
I fled paradise. I leapt through fiery air.

    Oscar dethroned.
    Oscar disowned.
    Gold turned to dross.
    Dross turned to dung
    When I was young.
    When I was young.

Poems 1991 – 98

Champp Dust

The tableau of me—MM, stepping out, remaindered, in my nite-club finery from Mount Shenandoah, ermine pit bull boa freshly Hollanderized. Hi guys. Reminded me. Hi guys. Peculiar lunge—of you, Lost Boy. Hunched over all gauche—clutching gloopy entrails "wha' won't stop emigrationing" —read-outs of what's to come: glistening configurations slipping through our fingers fast.

Chancre to twitch in the sun just a bit . . . like a rainbow trout on a glossy white wharf gasping its last, before blasting away into a star system of eternal flipper action and lip suction.

Gluttonous slumber munching. Varied dream coast surround.
Bottom line is:

> For breakfast, cat scam scene. Nah.
> I, Venus Wheatena.
> I, Venus maple syrup.
> I, Venus French toast.
> Queer rupture/rapture. "Cheer up"
> Sez infomercial ghost.

Relieving themselves before some Lenten whip session or
other. I'm just furious. Too soon consign Lost Boy to Has-Been
Never-Was slot. What with the proliferation of channels,
strain keep track what day Millennium it is, to put it crudely.
Religioso earphones have seared internal verities into our
patched noggins (non-compost mantras) while the jitzu, jitzu
potassium support group—Hi guys. V-day grope therapy so
soon? Cloacal smarm. Seems our worser 'arf palmed him off.
Infectoid stud tore bod to smithereens. Upshot. My papal
mouth dam awaits malpractice zoot suit. Legal conduit is now
offshore shell game. Fœtus excrement hurled by placebo
zealots musses where MM's head's at.

Me?
Happy surf's up.

▪ 3 ▪

The surround of the surround.
Number crunching's bottom line (banging shutter):
Lost Boy Fax.

Lost Boy Fax.
Bad break. Same old shit. Feeding frenzy. Virulent swirls
and winter gusts dump parasites. Fast-lane achievers
keep upping their bravado quotient. When I lost the
Scary Fairy Contest—everything went fast. Must share
bike to work.

Shabby Eyetalian sandals. Dago wop wop wop along the
factory floor glittery with industrial diamond dust.
Nights, I got crammed into a tiny hive hellhole. Stench
of upchucked barf—swamperama barf. No way, José, stay
purified of add-on Life-O-Matic Synergy. Sole liquidity
access, frozen lice jujube cubes, not pre-tested for chigger
embryos. Plus which they've melted.

We have all trudged barefoot to the laptop, partitioned.

Leathery fingers squeeze our balls till blue in the face.
Fucking border patrol! Have-not Zouave No-Goodniks
salivate at finding caches of smack inside sex toys, crates
of black phalluses for export to the indigenous ethnics of
the snowy buttes. Or five o'clock shadow Virgin Mary
He-Shes, squatting in the manger, blue lace lingerie hiked
up, indulging in non-procreative outercourse with hol-
lowed out Holy Babes, who scarf their lice jujube effluvia.

And such rich gorgeola Gregorian chants, Latin cadences
beautifully enunciated by the famous prancing reindeer
cadet corps imported from Guam, all the while myrrh wafts.

Darling Lost Boy,

I wish I could assist your aged go-go wolverine. Yikes!
The registration of the ventriloquists alone,
woofy woofy, the ennui since plastic duct axed.

LP of castor oil repartee glugs renders
The Instruction Manual impenetrable.

Impenetrable!
And how, just how, can I be expected to piece
DOA DOA DOA out the snarly mouthpiece?

Mmm. Love that palsy-walsy boogie-woogie MM
whisper you ape so perfectly! Prayeth hard I find
Holy Babe reject—pout too louche. May he land
at my feet, lift curse.

Want true-blue Lost Boy selfhood so bad.
Not some white bread escapee from
Welcome Wagon fag spotters.

■ 4 ■

Reminds me of a CIA contra flub I was peripherally
                        posing as go-go girlie-boy molested
        idyll Port-au
    back when Ike mole
                heavyset father figure
                        anal squirming under the Bunsen burner

            bacterial suction caps
        deadly flesh slicers
undesirables prettied up to pass for patinas, Executive Suite patinas

    medallions of land mines

            viral staircase solo

    zombie mongrel jissom flecks
                        splat into Ambassador Yao's
    snug-as-a-bug-in-a-dug fang implant

        rried out

            feet fir

Hi, guys. Thanks for waiting for the airless actionlessness to resume. Personal touch—moisturizer bubbled on the pubescent peach fuzz of Lost Boy's upper lip. Palaver over the bier— how inspire and mulct breadwinners in an epoch of woe and societal dysfunction. In my head, as happens, romantic film loop hunkers down. Stranger's embrace. Hard-on. His. Felt through pants. Meant for each other. Must pull together for this new love bliss! Not much time for improvements—tummy tucks and psychic high kicks—so as not disappoint him ere my errant member gallivants off in search of a hidden agenda— me gussied up as MM, him as Lost Boy.

Simple! MM and Lost Boy curl up on Power-Matic placemat which we all favor globally a bunch. The two lie there, flexing. Who they take down with them depends on the extent of the downsizing, architecturally disallowed, in our wellness mini-warehouse. Wellness may sound complex, but down the road it works.

While on done gone hold, let's us implode the flip side, mayn't we? Most appreciative of quality time. Home entertainment sex acts closed down—more undivvied focus. I must fix breakfast while I shove meditation suppositories into my benumbed and aftershocked orifices. My organs haven't worked the room right since Affray of Skunk's Misery. It still raises my hackles— Vasectomy Terroristes Clobber Hirsute Galoots.

Camouflaged as an iceberg, I hid out in Generalissimo Yao's meat locker, hung with shrouded game. Kept alert reshuffling my scanty priorities.

A) Spermatozoa zone depleted of Life Force zeitgeist. Why me?

B) King PermaFrost of 1937? I must ready acceptance speech in case. Memo—practice wafer insertion in the pelicans' beaks.

c) Disruptive clairvoyant powers. See crowded dance floor. Live orch. See skeletons with handbags. Toupees and silicon body parts. Snakelike Conga line.

Stop at once! Now! This second! I mean it!

Tangential observation craves in right here. Ever notice how nerve-ends bum out from too much third-sex-and-peacetime stress? If they could only dredge up primeval sap ill-rememberethèd, but they can't, barely able to whistle three bars of *Goofball Serenade,* la-di-dah dahlias, twue womance mollycoddling, hewn spoon non sequiturs easily adapted to same-sex reveries. I always dreamed of learning how to emit real rage at Kevin's Queer-as-Dick's-Hatband Uncle Brie, zonked in the catbird seat, hissing Beige Book homilies at hapless neophytes such as you and I! All of us'd, I warrant, refuse to git in a snit about his Bette Nwa Nwa we called her—stagflation gridlock in the Red Sea. Or maybe was it the Dead Sea? Or that Club Med on Mount Ararat where can, canib, cannabis, can something or other—strewn carrion, five minutes before the airship stuck together with Juicy Fruit docked. Why harangue the few remaining deconstructed dreamboats, taking up the cudgel for Ice Age plants and minerals too monolithic to be co-opted? Stick those marvels in detection dump sites on done gone hold. With psychological warfare loudspeakers that amplify fellatio slurps, wan joke worn thin, like a defective balloon can do farts, the harder you squeeze, till fingernail-on-blackboard piffle trails off. Continues to trail off till at long last screamy silence. Party's over. That'll larn 'em.

"Recycled paper lace?" MM hooted, her fingernails drumming against the kilted Scottie Puppy plastique plaid placemat. Lost Boy says rattlesnake skin so regenerative in Setzuan, must be ingested with raw ewe esophagi. Problem solved! We all went out to celebrate, danced the night away. Coituses too brusque —hoity-toity. Can't tolerate rearview mirror voyeuses.

Remaindered for the holiday season, taking up precious shelf space. We hadn't the heart to send MM to the pulpers in Taiwan for remolding as an egg-shaped old duffer.

Hi guys. Thanks for waiting for the actionless airlessness to resume. Seductive synthetics abound to replace them thar three squares. Today, I had my usual break-of-day intake. Dripped my Wheatena biopsy in record time. Expert consensus—whirligig snippets are whooping it up down in the tracts. Constant prowl for more fodder. If host killed, they kaput. It's that simple. Not easy find new palazzo, groaning sideboard well stocked with devourables—forget candelabras. Baked Alaska munchies served at room temp. Humpy footmen forbidden groin contact or "Have A Nice Day" solecisms, and (does anyone still read Emily Post?) after the ladies have repaired to the pergola, no soft porn reruns of MM funeral home Last Rites. Golly Grrr. This is so New Age—demotic muddle headlong, normal functions scrambled, role model expected to provide round-the-clock gangfucks to a horde of lithe scalawags—testosterone freeloaders, one and all. Only recourse is: move forefinger left to right across throat. Thus host signals: Time Go Home. Gasp their last in a welter of lunar craters—chaos theory still twittering away, its subtlety unhoned. Tribal hearsay: last breath wisp turns into an Amazon butterfly reputed to be extinct.

8

I recommend the fotos unequiv taste for choc flav lemo rinds

In the entrails, Skateboard Whiz, my shadow friend, has been trussed into an epoch of *vin ordinaire* and heartless individuation now all the rage among the hot male role models, street-smart but brain-dead. What the fusion magazine states: experts must come down harder on Lumpy Harriet and her ilk. Not ethical, spoiling quality time daylight hours. No safe turf now. Monsters of the Night penetrate the winter screens, infiltrate our personal watersports and take a dump on our never-to-be-fondled ensembles. Plus abscond with upscale exotica luxury items—Lamborghini Romeo & Yseult conversion vans to die for. They don't even have an operator permit or bother to design semiotic foreplay ads in their incomprehensible salt-mine dialect of verbless, nounless adjectiveless whimpers and grunts. But what really pisses me off (Lost Boy, Lost Boy, oh darling soulmate, forgive this hyper riff) is this—they won't help us develop a basic long-term strategy. Brood about this on rainy summer afternoons. I do feel oddly energized by mistaken identity Lost Boy mutants.

Energized by mirthquake brownouts. The scrape and clomp of a club foot on cobblestones is deranging as I sidle home with Lost Boy to our *pied à* terror, out on Pancreas Concourse. How can I be expected to further my spreadsheets of ruses and spiels about the Oud Countree and that glorious day, a masterpiece epiphany-wise, when I first met Lost Boy. Professional temple virgins swayed down the dirt road, imitating how the river meanders, not knowing its own mind. Lost Boy and I, strangers still, watched the priest strangle a chicken with his bare hands, and then poke at lustrous entrails in the dust with his ebony walking stick.

Bully show! River'll wet valley floor he says, but the bumper crop'll depress persimmon prices "mind sacs on empty" come 1964. Defective ventilation is killing off the warrior caste. He's so angry at factors beyond Gautama's control. A sad fate awaits each Persimmon Buddha bundled up in chic see-thru jammies to keep warm, expensively gift-wrapped for the glitterati and psyche-shapers, getting the job done in highrises across the ocean, each with its own private wellness laguna.

9

Heigh-ho. Gorged on pat of real Vermont butter, reward for working so hard to probe surtext above this, my new lingo code. Factoid for the talk shows—may not be readily apparent to the amateur sleuth, weaned on anthropomorphic sitcoms as I was —but I've been influenced viscerally by postmodern civilizbldng-blcks&tittydscntnts that form dangling parsings and phrenology graphics—i.e. meaningful up and at 'em head bumps. Over to you, contemporary spinoffs and recycled icons. MM Loop always breaks off here (intercom siren)—fortunately before I need incarcerate the lovely feminist verb *subsume* purged of raillery. Scared of release gong, fearing some verdict, social shift right disguised as social shift left, that will render my surtext too small-print for eyes accustomed to sky slogans in mufti—How To's that leave the spectator a better off ace in space, no trace etc. Diaghilev I'm not. What to do about the shrouded D, E snoozing behind the tormentor, A fornicating with T under the dropcloth, butoh H harnessed up in the flies for her awe-inspiringly butch descent into the pyre. Antsy dance sequence—the male athletes, the cavalry officers waiting in the wings. Their steroids are panting to crossover—white collar suburban discretionary income to fuck over good. They HATE *Einstein in the Botched Hut* slowness. Lost Boy emerges. Drinks glass of milk (cosmos). Scratches his haunch (Big Bang theory). Goes back in (Nam). Window lights up (Berlin Wall). Lobster appears (More Berlin Wall). Stares out (More Berlin Wall). Pulls down the shade with one claw (Christmas Dinner with Dick & Pat, Ron & Nancy). Big Deal! They have crowd control tools to market, franchises to endorse and carcinogenic residuals to deplore. The monkey troupe is restive, huzzahs and bananas long overdue. Essential I come up with nirvana apotheosis to validate The Howitzer Factory (Act One), Soil Tested Truck Garden (Act Two), and the Epilogue, set in a smalltown mall—Virgin of The Sequoia Deflowered. Then the fancy-dress free-for-all. President's Day fertility rite to herald the end of cabin fever fire sales. I promised Mr. Squeegee the little doll people'd be back in their circus dorm by midnight, circuitry intact. How can I keep funding this legion of topdrawer spindoctors working overtime? Their pilot projects shaped by consumer research, true, might make my half-dotty rantings *viable*—I think that's the right word, conjoined to *venue, name magic* and *deacquisitioned shelf life,* not in any particular order. Rewrites have plumb wore me out. Yesterday, I came up with *Sez infomercial ghost* as MM's exit line as she swandives off the gorilla's furrowed brow into the arms of . . . of . . . Urinal Sailor. Genre shifts here. Paycheck pissed away. Blond. Cute butt. Hot for nooky, cunt-mouth nooky. How to spirit MM into the men's (James Dean type) room, disguised as a sissyboy for the blowjob? Cut to tidal wave vs Moses screaming for help (Montgomery Clift), eyes gaga, end of all the paltry advances we hold so dear, nuance accretions, if/when coupled through the decades of TV snacks, sin taxes, shaggy dog stories with punchlines now consigned to oblivion. Genre shifts here. Special effects. Wiped out. Alien blobs squirm through mudflats, evolution reversal, back to amœbic platitudes, shoveling in raw pollywogs and condom flotsam, hole cost spinning out of control, black hole cost, oh and how the dole went out of fashion as falling through the cracks came in, anemic gratitude, cracks now deep-sea abysses of techtonic violence, with tangled tentacles at rest on the ocean floor. My heart goes out to all flimflam buffs, me included, yearning for deliverance so seamless, it must seem of an ageless timelessness, names changed out of dread of the litiginous living. Work-in-progress, remember. This morning's treatment looks fine, ready to roll. Outfielder stares at the ball so fixated he doesn't even hear his teammates, his fans in the stands, screaming in anguish at his weirdo conduct. So entranced, he doesn't crane to see MM, still fondling her jewelry in a rose-hued cloud, dusk now, a cloud turning flesh purple, walloped and bruised flesh purple, as she sings, exit line to Lost Boy, wherever he is, "Enjoy your night."

Bare Bones

It was love at first sight, on the Staten Island ferry.
I'm part of an anti-Nam Poet Protest he and Ted come to.

We collaborate. He artist, me words.
Me, poet-librettist reduced to comic strip balloons?
It's a ruse, to be with him.

He has his weird side.
Two shrimp cocktails, that's his main course.

Our first tennis date.
Interrogated closely, he assures me he plays well.
He can't even hit the ball.
I curse my luck.
I've fallen for a dysfunctional mythomaniac.

We undress.
His mysterious undergarment fascinates and scares me.
It hangs loose from his bony arms, skinny torso,
The hunchy back he's so ashamed of.
Raggedy yellow loops.
Waif Macramé.
Dleam Come Tlue.
My Very Own Urchin Savant.

Only he isn't mine.
Triangle. Jealous anguish.
Oh, the searing yearning.

I put my foot down.
Triangle tapers off.
Just us two, sort of.

Gray areas.
Nights off.

He's late for dinner.
I probe, against our code.
He explains, innocent of the merest shred of guilt,
Surprise outside sex plus small talk takes time.
High ground fury, nowhere to go.
Chastened, I heat up the meal.
We eat.
In bed, we share Champale.

He's big on holidays. All holidays.
Even Groundhog Day.
A-Day stands for Anniversary Day—our first night.
Holidays mean gifts.

His core belief, Gypsy source:
Be rememberethéd for what thou givest,
Seeking nothing back,
Except the pleasure giving gives.
He raises gift-giving to a noble art,
As finely honed,
As viewer friendly as—
His Art.

He gives me
The Dolly Sisters
In pastel sailor drag.
Art Deco statuette.
I'm appalled.
Initially.
Slowly he teaches me to give up
Received "good taste."

His recurrent dream:
Finding jewels,
Buried jewels.
We begin exchanging rings.
Every Xmas.
Birthdays.

He makes me necklace collages.
Charms. Enamels.
A cluster, minuscule photos of him,
In miniature glass lockets with glass fronts—
His face and naked body parts.
Surefire way to get touched at parties, he points out.
As if the gift weren't enough.

He stutters.
Low voice, can't make out his words.
Bend close. Tulsa accent.
E becomes I.
Pinitintiary.
Pass me the pin.

I hand him wine lists,
So I can hear him wrap his stutter
Around Pouilly-Fuissé.

His spelling.
Eccentric phonetic. A hoot.
Printed Block Upper Case.
I'm his checker, see his writings first, thrilling perk.

His mental geography maps are surreal.
Australia is in Europe.
Venice is its capital.

Europe honeymoon.
Spoleto Poetry Fest. Rome airport.
I panic. Train sked, how, station where?
My sensible beloved rescuer cuts through the problem.
Taxi.
Taxi.
From Rome Airport to Spoleto.
And subsequently from Madrid to Granada.
And subsequently everywhere in foreign lands.

Pre-Armani, he hates jackets and ties, wears jeans,
White shirt unbuttoned way down to reveal his chest mat,
So teen-age cute, Gian-Carlo Menotti takes me aside,
Festival Du Monde! Hustlers are a no-no!

Explain he's an A List Genius?
Flash our first collab, *The Baby Book?*
Quote blurbs?

Frank: "The most peculiar thing I've ever read."
Andy: "Fantastic! Fantastic!"
Ron: "The greatest book of all time."

I dummy up.
Kowtow. *Ciao* Spoleto.

Our M.O. evolves.
Four months together in Vermont.
June to October.
Rest of the year, delicate but tenacious bonds.
We cohere, summer to summer,
Despite cæsuras, rifts and dumpings,
Once each, luckily staggered.

In hosp, he mentions we've lasted thirty-one years.
In hosp, he says he thinks of us as married.
In hosp, he says I'm doing better than he expected,
Dealing with the circles of hell
He's descending deeper and deeper into:
Narrowing options,
Enveloping pain.
In hosp, he says we've been faithful.
We've had a good life.

Proud moment.
We're at Naropa.
Allen beseeches, cheer up poor old lonely old Burroughs.
Dead flesh eyes don't waste a sec on me,
Start to sparkle with reptilian lust.
Allen says: "Bill, they're a couple."

Bad times.
His new lover, wily dominatrix,
Sneaks up on us both.
Speed.

Thirty something, I swell, take dex.
Share fifty-fifty
This Ted drug he's used since his Tulsa teens.
Blissful bond, enabling dex togetherness.
How brilliantly he works,
Long hours a snap.
Esthetic micro-management other artists would kill for.
Protean quantity, star quality,
As his last Fischbach smash proves.

I cross the abyss.

His city studio is a madhouse of mounds,
Color-coded, red here, yellow there,
Raw material screaming
Collage me,
Collage me,
Turn me into jewels.

I partake of the white powder, his lover.
We try to collab.
The Way We Were.
Nada. Nada.
It's the black pit.
I flee.

He comes out of it on his own.
Wishy-washy, not all there,
Back together in Vermont,
He tries to make art.
Lays out his brushes upon arrival.
Settles for reading, nonstop reading,
Barbara Pym his summer standby.

He-as-artist rematerializes fully, once.
For me: *Sung Sex* drawings,
Boy in bed odalisques,
Abstractions, spare Japanesey lines,
Lola my cat,
Whose Fancy Feast he fluffs up meticulously,
Mornings, first thing,
Whose white hair he patiently picks off
Armani jacket and pants.

He holds these new drawings in low esteem.
Tiptoes away
From the casino paradise
Art Biz gulag.
Closes shop.

His first retrospective.
University, San Diego.
Hung thuggishly, as if for a cineplex lobby.
I hate to see his work sloughed off this way.
How must he feel?

Despite snake oil panaceas,
His hair recedes. Salt and pepper.
Small bald spot I can't get enough of.
Jowls. Older eyes. Gym biceps. Kid thin.

A first. *Quel horreur,* his face turns into Nixon.
A Now-See-Now-Don't magic trick of time.
One visual he must never never know of.

He loves to see old couples holding hands,
Has-beens on TV with food-on-the-table jobs,
Worries how the young, droopy pants, obnoxious dyes,
Must terrify The Old.

We start seeing Edwin Denby, replica perfection,
Suited and tied, mannerly gait,
Downtown Montpelier epiphany.
Talisman of all the time in the world,
This recurrent mirage of resurrection from death,
An omen of quirky survival.

The first plague death: Bill Elliott.

On the way to dinner one night,
I bring up lovemaking, death risk.
I think I'm thinking of my own survival.
What I don't dare think is:
Unwittingly becoming
The instrument of his death.

We become companionate.

Test.
I'm OK.
Privacy transgression, I ask.
He's OK.

He tells me he has AIDS.
The how, not the when.
In Vermont, he can't tan.
The sun is lethal.

He reads, reads, reads all the time.
Cartons from "Three Lives" are never enough.
He shoulders more of the domestic daily round.
What I've always wanted happens.

He takes care of me more.
We take care of each other.
A balance achieved.
We're content together.

Which I should have been prepared for.
He always comes through,
Makes the best of the crisis situation.

When Jimmy uproots
Whole beds of flowers,
Starts washing money,
J.A. (hapless guest) and snit-prone I
Turn into Joan Crawford parodies,
Wide-eyed at full moon psychopath
Clomping up the cliffhouse stairwell.

He takes command.
Talks Jimmy into the waiting police car.
As he once released John Wieners
From restaurant rant, accusatory pointing,
"You're the Mayor of Boston's wife,
        Boston's wife, Boston's wife."

And far back, me.
Pyschodribble whinings. Labyrinthine snarl.
Analysand mind spill.
Sweet calm of acceptance: come as you are.

Car crash.
Totaled.
In shock.
He gets up, sees if other car's driver's OK.

June, '93. I have diabetes.
My new better half takes charge.
No nonsense trainer,
Gentle carer, patient restorer,
Walks me, pushes me,
Further, further.

I'm his good child, eat right.
Drop 40 pounds by summer's end.
Sugar plummets to normal.
Balm of good sense, end of no win.

His insides act up.
He goes to hosp.
Comes back too weak for walks.
Our last October.

He accepts the unacceptable.
Where does such deep grace come from?

We discuss our respective deaths.
Ashes,
Field uphill,
Us both.
Ashes scattered.
Flesh ash, bone ash,
One day commingled,
Under white pines,
An enclosure Ron calls druidic.

In NYC
All fall and winter and spring,
He weakens.
On May 25th, late afternoon, he dies.
In June, his brother John
Gives me his ashes.

By a white quartz boulder,
Under protective pines,
I scatter Joe Brainard's ashes.

Promise kept.

Closure.

Remembrance

Animals in the Walls

They snack on olden underpinnings,
joists and cement,
news wads,
urine spattered lists of the lost:
tempests, plagues,
forests in Belle France.

Famine,
inches from my noggin
abob in its ocean sky.
Diaspora vertigo.

Dogs. Black mouths.
What color the tongues, I ask you.
What color the tongues?

White fur hot from heat.
The other sigher in the room.
Constant Red Eye Alert.
Transit nonspecific.
Tracks'll converge. Cumulus'll billow,
hiding dancing feet.
Yo, you. Welcome home, old party.

Couth south.
White pines sough. Hummingbirds rippety rip,
stub their beaks on poppies painted on
federally funded cinderblock windows:
Boulevard of Loco Screams.

Downy ZZZZs. On mossy coverlet, me.
Pretty please, comely lover. Let me. Let me.

Spring in Argentina

Dream repeat. Sob heart out on mat. Joe lost.
In transit, new nudo pseudo-Significant o
on small boat with me. Many passengeros.

Where do dream strangers come from?
Verismo extras. Unstoppable composites.

Real life stalks my operatic crises.
My part still unwritten on Opening Night,
everyone but me has their lines down cold.

      Curtain never rises.
Boat never lands.
      Desayuno.
Fear of pandemic future swept under.

Local Branch

Sun, wind, gamma wavelengths, wind, sun.

Luscious disarray thrusts out, up and at 'em.
They natter away, fending off devourers whatever their tech.

Calipers have categorized zillions of odor lingos,
filaments with rhythmic dialects you and I'd kill for,
survival subterfuges experts still file under GUNK.

Database in superb shape despite cutbacks. Warehoused.
I can attest the last oral willpower ode just went off camera—
how to eke out a leg-up when I sleep cruddy, the Fed.
I chowdown good, piss on the grass, shit razorblades A-OK.

Banner years unimpeded. Ike. Nike. Spike: impregnable urns!
Icons now. Along with the *Götterdämmerung* chirpage/frottage
of a humpy summer day, laid out nice and linear,
priced per pop in that *Satevepost* print ad,
the week the ocean of sepia tears dried up.

Interestingly enough, factoid ground into the muck.
Us contrarian romantics, who still hone each last shred
of self-glow, picture it frozen in time, quid pro quo:
The Dawn Salute, even the mingiest tendril color-coordinated.
Failsafe infrastructure intuited his/her crowd control,
robotic timbre of pre-have-a-nice-day-unisex grunt perfect.

His/his her/her best case scenarios (I love 'em! I love 'em!)
still on the drawing pad, like me—perpetual trainee, mute,
ogling the goings-on through a Vaseline-smeared lens.
Nutso as a leaf, prelit, posed. That very night, Zía,
ex-Miss Suisse, stalked out of my life. Real huffy slalom.

Scenery in the driver's seat infuriates flabby beauty.
Hairy greed for zee possible eez no match for primordial
Herr Field & Señorita Hedge, Cousin Gully & Uncle Tumbleweed.
Yet another stalemate dream I woke up from, undumped.

But safe, my daily dozen to squeeze past. Silly mounds to trim,
abode of skunk to skirt. The gathering of the clan at dusk.
Toke. Small talk. Stalin's double died. The pond a pond.

Not dried mud flat, in chunks, with cracks skittering crazily,
terminal chaos, a parody of city planning run amok.

Clambered back up to the wavelengths. Took eons, seemingly.

Jakarta Night Arrival

Doktor Gigi, adorable practitioneress,
shingle spang on the Equator,
my poopoo has me middling troubled.
Immensity of Bod Fat. Sugar Futures,
bringdown I dislocate from postmodern matrix.

Why you not share calm zoom, Dok Gigi,
cabin hum of my airbus cocoon?
Update. Poofter left hand now good as new.
All gone, palm pain. Fingers kittenish!
Right hand fresh for love signal test squeeze
from chance bonanza of fulsome beauty.

I eye-molest ox-slow bamboozled,
visual lotería, win-win site of tropical exotica.

I eye-engorge roadside flux. Erotic peopledness.
Stilt-home verandahs, shantytown languors.
Luscious eye-rape swoon, all longings fulfilled.

Eye-rape see-thru nano-instant,
animal know-how of pounce, gobble,
roadkill remains an eternity toy.

Earlobe curve, nape diaspora.
Elegant crotch scratch. Promo?

Mustn't deconstruct vine overhang tangle.
No cave guff, prehistory haunch malarkey.

Futurist highrise neon obfuscates
Golden Happy Sarong Boy Moon.

Squatter burbs squeeze khaki rivers.
Night air flood-sodden.
Parfum de Gym Sox.

Why this detritus?
So much clutter when I now old?
Say why, Doktor Gigi? Yes why.

Sunday in Dunedin

Took guts, that Sunday in Dunedin, 1933, to go on strike.
Beef up the search-and-destroy tincture spray?
      Us crossdressers balked.
      The royal birthrate went off its nut.
      Our runway lolly dove.

Polka dot maternity jammies were deemed *posh toff*.
Svelte glitter vogueing, *au contraire* . . . why bellyache?
Spindly leaf scratches had aged oh so distressingly
our ecosystem of dry turds and mountain stream freshets,
which, to this day, drip and drip, drop by stingy drop.
Bully! Soon to be deactivated. We transvestite extremists outed
how the resultant s-s-s-stench (excuse anxiety sibilance)
of granitic worry lines breeds corrosive memory gaps—
onslaughts prettified, capitulations ossified ad nauseam.

Squiggle of erasure here. Info niche parameters upheld.
Property values of the Living Dead—Shaddap, Griselda.

Best I renege, not harp on the nasty rabbit business.
Rabbit I mistranslated as *rabid Arab*.
Bad body mike. My first pink slip. The Big If is this:
how retrieve my personal archive from Ruby Hollywood
aka Collin Montrose iii, okra and obelisk heir?

    "From fag hag paranoia to Guam fortress mentality,
    her lineage of legitimate dissent and descent
    ends up miniaturized, a blurry swale
    of burgeoning op ed vagaries
    and Peel-Me-A-Banana-Bwana miasma.
    If you mean muff-dive, say muff-dive."

That's Ruby, critiquing my spiritual atrophy. True,
decades-long tenterhooks have crosshatched my edgy sheen.

1986. Five strong, Boss Sis, us. Feminist collective
donned its doughty khaki puttees. Back On Strike.
Girding our abandoned kiosk, we chanted imprecations,
stonewalled dilutive icons, Empire Twaddle.

How I loved Plop O'Nuggets' resuscitated hand-me-downs!
Charmingly soiled torn lace (grease-stained antimacassars)
for windshield wipers, oxbow patterned, to lean against.
Propped up, they took all the Original Settler settees, they did.

About the narcissistic rabbits. First, wedged in, more outing.
My résumé for devout sixth graders: *Why I Gotcha Transvestite.*
A baby boy in a girl's body, I was tormented by spindly leafage.
These trees come from the same supermarket superpower
(cringe at mention) I derive from. Purportedly. West Coastiana.
Along with gold rush fever, phone sex, and Madame Blavatsky.

Class dismissed. My next truth lode: drug-free mood ameliorator.
Caveat. The below-mentioned force fields are impedimentia
to "giving up the Millennium Ghost" 1997 style, 99% unobserved:
       A. Rabbit City.
       B. Sis Boss Kiosk.
       C. General Strike Co-opted.
       D. Ooga-Ooga Beluga.
       E. Wrong Way Pincer Ejac—

Today, from my granary synchronicity vantage point, C is correct.
I'm staring implacably at a windowless building's exhaust pipe.
Womb conjectures well up—ethnic diaspora yarns.
How they plagued our one remaining in-law in Brno!

Impeccably updated,
generational pile-up intact,
how explain the one loophole?
Dmitri Emsiggi, wastrel turncoat.

Archbishop Emsiggi's vial of stolen wolf spittle cracked,
spattering its alchemical cornucopia on the cobblestones.

Penniless, we sailed for Dunedin, blood lust a lost art.

Honest, I only gained admittance after the reverbs got sloppy—
quavery as-if-underwater query bubbles
starring a one-eyed tyrant.
My stand-in, his victim, scampered to safety
under floorboards. In the tunnel, *my* turn,
I sang my first "predicament" ditty.
That day, after chapel, I peed into our mud room spittoon.
My boyhood omniscience bloomed and dried.
Singular instant.

Outside, blitzkrieg arrows fucked and thickened, impregnated.
Vacation over, my main focus was my telephone pole total,
added to daily via autobus excursions.
I fended off misery voids. Two samples.
        Piano keys moving up and down of their own accord.
        "Pass the canapés, Lloyd."
Thus was my invisibility bliss invariably shattered.

Precursor of rabbit zillions, I learned to conjure up dark places,
moist earth to press against, under a bush shaped like a head,
its fœtal human face grinning between clenched orifice lips.

Welcome Home
—for CW

Grappling tenderly with a plenitude of unknowns,
joy reigns, as I dally, between laps, in Yoomee Lake,
awaiting the unmet you, the unseen you I long to love,
untethered from paper shape of muse missive, phone click,
secreted in the buoyant fastness of my upland boondock.
Tiny fish mouths nibble my old guy puckered jewels,
duped by testosterone attar of lost boyhood, museum quality,
buffeted by wave spume/wind shear patterns.
The Major Hoople of my fortress mind-set is on sick leave,
discombobulated by the luxuriance of my fleshly imaginings—
our first double dare, coupling in the Enchanted Haunted Forest.
Next. Head home, past squeaky-clean creation myth conundrums.

     Problematic. You keep opening me up.
     Freed from time-clock strictures,
     sequestered from cause-and-effect,
     role reversals blur boundaries.

     Ah, lucky you-and-me. Rescue operation.
     We've been gerrymandered irreversibly,
     into a dream map shape, us, unanimous.
     From Yoomee Lake to this miracle zone—
          Destiny, salud!

     A frontier home,
     with unforeseeable trajectories
     hungry for our roots.

     Welcome, my love,
     to a terra firma
     up to us to find.

Rummage Sale
—for CW

7 PM. Visual dossier of high-rise ruses, reflected.
Line of mountain range under pale sky
truncated by beige-white skyscraper stripes:
Laundry (misread) Insurance Bldg.
Triggers fantasy—malpractice, Orlon chiffon
discoloration recompense, status pratfall,
hooted at, opprobrium malaise. Civilization.
Burgeoning enterprises fatten up massive gray areas.
Document shredder truck glimpsed earlier. A *truck!*

City centrum: October Daylight Saving spring.
Dying antipodal sun enters left via
black glass oval. Panel panoply, row upon row.
Immersion into red taillights aswim.
Traffic streams aslant defy death and linear rectitude,
update silent movie car chases, sight gags,
sight gags going nowhere fast. Stop-'n'-Start norms
so sportive and loony. Midair showbiz. Mirror
Sun exits behind panel cloud, chiaroscuro zone
out of sync with swart pre-night expanse overhead.
Harbor sliver real water where Brit debtors dumped,
paltry and unreal amid real estate legerdemain.

Now lost to view. Monolithic night now.
Visible behind the panels: spanking new work stations.
Graveyard shift moves about. Sits, plugs in to noon
yesterday on Wall Street. Some floors never close.
Me too. Retreat to bed, reading matter.
I leave ITT Auckland Sheraton curtain as is.
Hotel Lautréamont by John Ashbery.
Perfect fit. Quality Time. STET.

Panopticon for Calamity Winifred

Fighting for breath under blood-red Mama Uterine foam
in hostile takeover mode. Abyss dread abated by ironic shrug
at narco-syringe. Poor twerp. Just another old worthy undone
by A) *Ectoplasm Spillage*—shopworn toxicity of ghost hug,

Twister Bea's asparagus wobble suffused the maw of August dusk,
rancid from wetsuits, yahoos in spa pools dunked.
Rotten egg fart blips on temp hold. BCD & E—forget it.
I'm thine, my love, multiple-choice Fate skunked.

But your promontory micro-manages my islet sump'n awful.
Scads of insights (shared satori)—I recall that much.
Then you bent down like a corkscrew to retrieve the tin ladle,
though loath to chug-a-lug health broth, duo-style. Crutch:

busy ourselves with grouse/douse/spouse/Bauhaus symbiosis.
Fun hone scimitars of mole bone, schmaltzy flecks omniv STOP!
Present potent? Iffy juncture. Nature/nurture so naughty-nice.
Bare-assed that noon, I crossed Granite Plaza. Web command: HOP

TO IT. IT consists of eunuch barrage—high IQ drivel. Worsens
sensory impoverishment, ups vagrancy. My new union of norm
and derring-do invalidates such morality implants. Reduces guff.
Bankruptcy ploys not so piss-in-mouth. Back home (barn dorm),

flashlight at the ready, spotlit kinky sex scenes. Formulaic, yeah,
but the promised porn classics got born again last Ozzie & Harriet Day
as virgin surf foam, components a-swirl, arcane directives macerated.
No free clinch the upshot. I pay. You pay. We all pay. Repay. Repay.

Amid the profit-and-loss rustle of nightfall, desert vistas open up.
So far, managing to outwit cheesy panaceas all a-glitter on the crags.
Only natural feel dispossessed. Aha! Post-coital hums defy doomsday.
Marginal flummery's gonna sneak us past encircling time lags.

Outback Taunt

—for Ann Lauterbach

. I .

Wild peach tree indicates way to Geisha Sea.
Flummoxed by the stress of racial reasoning,
A's buried persona staged a lurid turnabout geste,
a tad mingy colonial: baksheesh web of lamented mud
roiled. A lazy forewarning. Too late, granted.
At dawn, A'd faxed her Herr & Fraulein Mental Hygiene
how rain was tap-tap-tapping at the sand,
opening up a grid with a slamdunk lifestyle all its own,
a tee-many-Martoonis-hit-the-sack-Beelzebub maelstrom.
On the funerary dais, slouchers randy from memory loss
blathered about the trick rucksack's love smarm,
on exhibit in the futures pit. Its poop deranges the herd. Why?
Caveat. If noxious fumes, substitute *redneck studs* for *herd*.

Well now, the deli scion's realty ears really picked up on *gorse*
(slut noun)—from jissom to hang-ups to wax museum ritual.
Put another way: from bedlam to moisturizer to foreboding
of death flux, à la the night thoughts of a sci-fi mummified gland.

How they'd tempt A's shelved and bewildered oaf-self,
beloved of the *tabula rasa* elf-oaf, prehensile grifter,
whimpering in the supermall parking lot, rental compact lost,
desperately trying to visualize Greer, Greer Garson,
Greer Garson embattled, how she spilled salt, had to,
story board made her, on her heaving cleavage, specks,
white specks for Clark Gable to lick away cavalierly,
only he wouldn't do bed tongue. That flick never rolled.

■ 2 ■

If fodder spleenwurst,
risk-reward ratio silver spoon, A & I opine—
Boom/Bust clout.
Taunt heft empowers our desiccated siblings,
busy remaindering remnants of scanty longings.
Not mad! Quite correct,
given the given of "erratum belongings" denial.

Well now.
Starve out the tropics!
All laid out in the cover letter:
how a teensy-weensy sunspot
ends up engulfing lunar surflessness.

Interjection. Serious money.
Guru Gal's lost bijoux. Tomb fluff—
From Spasms under the Palms to Alms under Dead Elms.

All A shares is the silhouette line of rocks, worn out, curt.
She likes finding herself, surmise, visually molested, sort of,
a teenager again, in a witty quaalude desert, butted in on,
Last Chance Roadhouse butted in on, sort of,
where never-beens diss the bosky barmaid butted in on,
in a Tex-Mex hell, a kind of nowhere delta butted in on, sort of.

■ 3 ■

"O please sir, forgivableness! Llama is sufferings
horridly!" Subtext: tone of woebegone coup d'etat,
gang aglay. (If that doesn't work for you, try rough fun—
razor slices air above Venusian Elvis.
Male nude. Stilled balls.)
Stilled, the white pennant of the War Zone's ark.

Infusion of content. "Global security's what the wanton bitch . . ."
Embers now, fag end, limp lisp, sinks into the sofa, pooped.

Wading in the Everglades, hunting lost *bijouterie,*
Theda Bara nostrils a-quiver, weakens, weary of lust.
Iris of me, dead to the insect thrum in the briar patch.

Based on real life, this next segment, excised, zeroes in
on how I try to scare up a chilly-assed chimera d'amour,
in a blip-your-whip disco VCR of hardhats singing
Twisty Guy Duo Sniffin' Poppers.

Won't wash, these serious little lies that pick at us nitwits,
seeking lithe youth. My sked meant it this time. It? My It
leased hosiery, via Gus, for A's penthouse leap. Knotted.
Window ledge. Sink and you *will* sink, float down to the reef.

Our gender-neutral engine, togetherness embodied, flipflopped
last Baby Day. Kewpie dolls trended up. 'Twas the iddle pout,
attack wattage outwitting the sticky wicket of cope strategies.

Saga, from cinderblock cell to Sierra Madre high-rise—
rapid yaw. Scary tunnels'll, guesswork, blockade A's vita.
Her roots'll hyperventilate, shuffle off to stifled no,
temp no, no final nay say.

Peddle (i.e. ram down) camera obscura status quo dirt.
Haughty me! I articulate my dilemmas so cogently,
how to insure aperture crannies' rinsing and befouling,
how to variegate (out with it!) lissome writ large,
protracted commitment to swab and devour,
mop up, replenish. How to—if bungled?
Rephrase simply,
if/when
eye hollow.
Bye for now.

Forty Sonnet

Minus oinks, a shiny life of pollen feats awaits you.
Atchoo. Your new gene splice has defused the awful coming attractions.
Xylophone joined at the groin to Aunti Deli, Bubi, Kerenski, and Molli.
"I am so very happiest in my velveteen armchair, coasting through Bismark,
N.D. to the flashlite butte, batteries included nirvana. All lit up.
Eisenhower in his sky-blue Fury, patting Mamie's matching snood."

Click. Conga, remember? Then Dime Fallen Into Sea (what sea?) Pang.
Home. Survival Mall. The Yackety-Yack Kibitzers Fugue. Ask not what ye . . .
Eyrie. Stuck in the glass bell, Morty the Mortician's fingernail scratches
RRHIC. You've surmounted a gigantic peer victory, fore'er free of
Nada Dada stress, and the aye-aye russet shore dating back to womb
Of glacial ice, volcanic ash. Stone Age riffs, whammies and improvs.
Fizzy days are here again. Revivified the lost éclair. Youth my myths scuttled.
Fizzy days. Your very own diorama. Pink tinsel, luscious moon shadows.

Fiscal Nonsense

—for Jimmy Tampubolon

If I go back down Memory Lane.
When money was dirt cheap,
tongue-tied,
I ... I ...

Poor little rich kid balderdash, pipe down!
Company's expected—Officialdom,
and my witness protection cover-up isn't pat yet.

Dime-store forays.
Inexplicable crib death.
Cream was EL CREAM-O.

Keeping it straight unshitfaced a hassle—
remembrance spiel of fictive splurges.
Escape hatch: act *non compos.*

Familial Cordon Sanitaire clung to
must be flushed into the outback sinkhole,
down by the skeletal fairground,
sky rides freshly shrouded hulks.

The way I was was banished by Silent Shadow,
goody-goody second self off the couch, fecal.
Hoity-toity refugees poured in that war year,
skulked on benches, clots along the frowzy Esplanade.

What we do truly recall is
a grim contingency plan swallowed whole,
our first cocoon, an improv
devoid of restive day-night to-and-fro gusto,
a Safety First device
empowered by Graeco-Roman symmetry.

A bubble space, from which it was easy to see chimera mascara,
blind-eye thigh-high. Further up, God lipstick and Yahweh rouge.
Mystery is how wisps flake off. Chameleons disemboweled?

Once, pubescent genetic piffle unformed,
not a care in the world,
I glimpsed a pink smoke halo.
A solar eclipse dumped it, prehistory,
somewhere in lozenge-green Antarctica
on an extant iceberg still lost out there.
Ultra-violent (sic) ozone hole
the culprit, Pop sez. Said. Good ol' opinionated Pop.
"Ricochet of death ray, dearth hurrah, debt hooray!"
So went his revanchist consensus, spent.

Up we earthlings craned, shielded.
I prayed hard for more fadedness,
via quasi-legit contraband,
springtime gush of lunar spume.
Freshet from the Sea of Tranquility,
dutifully winterized froth. Ice lace.

I'm convinced adult downhill started with Lap Envy-
itis. Murderous aftermath, my id its captive jellyfish.
Why did I yearn so for Coming Attractions overkill?
Roseate dreammate, rhythmic? Revenge: vegetate.

Circumnavigate seasonal sameness.
Mindless niceties kept boring up from within.
Awoke, gabberflasted by sensuous midnight hush,
dead volcano working overtime.

Excuse please, now I take nice break from unbearable stress.
Doc Spin, your turn add on stick-ins to calm my variant multiselves.

Filler. Nostalgia filler. Shelve inconsequential nostalgia filler.
Failure. Shelve inconsequential go-go. Americana go-go. Failure.
Failure. *Tourist Cabin*. Joke hoax brands in joke *Icebox*. Failure.

Honbun, come glam Kweeny Quiche Puns Musee.
Its odor-free neon dims gross star ice muss.
Rinky-dink hue, writ ladylike vermillion. Cursive.

O KEESH ME KWEEK
O KEESH ME KWEEK
O KEESH ME KWEEK

The O blink. The K blink. The E blink.
Zapped so slow "EEK!"
screeches Plastique Freak,
phantasm geek.
Bites off styrofoam chickenoid head.
Ugly Beauty tug-o-war
where penguins once nodded out.
Reef end of loop.

Moral: free speech guarantees don't stop soul theft.
So, Hey Babe, let's all dipsy doodle Kweeny Quiche.
Kweeny Quiche Puns Musee Infomercial.

Time to rev up the chainsaw.
May Day chagrin. On call, snoozed my heyday away.
Mired. Sandstone jaw has receded bad. Wind.

Forgot to mention Spiro Agnew bit the dust.
All Price Chopper heliport flags at half-mast, nationwide.
My first pseudo-Howdy Doody Veep Death.
Goofy red letter day,
eh, Daisy Mae?

This next part's hearsay. I awoke, womanized, solo in a coma,
insensate . . . swamp . . . vamp afloat on a festive slagheap now extinct.
Coppery . . . frilly . . . such was the shrewdness of the bird colonies.

Dimwit treatment. How I love its elegiac lack of denouement!
Fallback crest—us temps trudge along surf fury, faces averted.
Hotsy-totsy contact high, neophyte schoolboy fingers interlaced.

Transition. Cloverleaf triple bypass. Hip, rub-a-dub nape fuzz,
its glint, golden glint, scarified glint link a sunrise rite.
Hiatus here. Babytalk hiatus. My height-weight trussed up.

"Sky ate us" my one riposte.
What's Yours and Mine ends up all Its.
Visceral hubbub—your menagerie—

SQUEEGEE KIWI

Primal squeak. Goners,
voicing their harum-scarum anthem,
exponential explosion.
Mental lists of lost memorabilia.
No more back-up. Jettison inessentials.

Press START.

[250]

Rid of survivor guilt, famished, I scanned the arid shore.
Promised and prepaid, earthquake-proof nutrients and housing
nowhere on the screen. Inland, too soon, blossom-strewn,

it's Lilac Time. Eerie. Afar, freebie view.
Frantic growths piss and moan, inches away,
lashed by silly-billy feelers, budding amok.

Merciless déjà vu cycle ends where it began—remote control.
There are worse dooms. Abandonment. Freeze-frame terror of same.

Solo itinerants, like me, expecting surcease, conjoined, who, you,
dot the crescent beach. Dot. Dot. Dot. Dash. Is all it is. All it is.

Decode?
Agreed.
Diminuendo of surprise expertise.
How-to cook the books
and gyp the fizz.

Happy Re-Return

■ I ■

Cost inefficient, my manic abandonment panic upgraded
Orphan *Doppelgänger Tango*. Our second celebratory spring hath
Recycled the me manacled to ancillary bunk, bare bones hidden.
Not possible? Vital organs in working order, I'm a healed temp. At
Ease, thanks to front burner mantra: Resume Human Form.
Liszt *"nize boy. 'Twaz outa angzt he engorged Zapoleon."*
I . . . I'll try bit o' aging procedure next. Down to cases. Ep. Epi—
Stamp (neglectoid) needs a good licking by grizzled sea captain.

WASMS—portmanteau pantoums you hurled into lingo shredder.
Odor of decay. So. Let's do it. Escape Prison Isle Isms. Epith—
Lured by the fussbudget hive's be-all of infra-light? Not me!
Fuck off! My roaring blood *hoorde ik mijn weem hapt weder*—
Rambling in foreign tongue, sticky-fingered, holy-moly.
And you? You? Just do it. What are we waiting for? Epithal—
Mumble. Slaphappy lambie-pie mumble Byzantine. Patience.

■ 2 ■

St. Ives is a rapids full of lively innocence. Can't go there.
Wakoski, Eshleman. Hoover. Levertov. Can't go there.
El Dorado, recall nodding acquaintance. Plant Dutch cress.
Tang piquant. Remind me, have some on me. Leaves don't keep.
Ziggurat shape. Love z. Hot for z. Want end wander Zuider Zee.

· 3 ·

Very jittery. *Ocean Immobile* topical message unit. Arcane.
Already over-committed. Teetery pile-up of values. Frontal
Nudity verboten. Verboten, this pantoumepithala—

Me, um, no deadbeat despite laughing stock enjambments.
I did pay for my own sieve hoax, traumatized awful, by La Boo.
Diaphanous Frenchie swamp goo-goo Gods curl me up fatal.
Die alone. Orphan fate, whomped. I meant: curl me up fetal.
How to downsize as co-waifs. Swing and sway and we'll do OK,
Light years apart. Inches away—the schtick of eons,
Afflatus deconstructed. Postmoderns, besnouted, gaze at us.
Rest in peace, shitheads. Springtime births great bone decor.

Acknowledgements

INTRODUCTION

The John Ashbery comments are from "The Figure in the Carport," Parnassus v.5 #1 (Fall/Winter), 1976, pp. 326–330.

POEM SONGS

Music by Kenward Elmslie: "Air," "Bio," and "Eggs" (poem title: "At The Controls"), "Sin in the Hinterlands," and "Sneaky Pete" (poem title: "Glittering Skyline") "And I Was There" (poem title: "Experts at Veneers"), and "Meat."
Music by Ken Deifik: "Bang-Bang Tango."
Music by John Gruen: "Adele The Vaudeville Martinet."
Music by Steven Taylor: "Girl Machine."

SONG LYRICS I

Music by Claibe Richardson: "They," "Brazil," and "One Night Stand."

From *Miss Julie*, an opera.
Libretto by Kenward Elmslie, based on the play by Strindberg.
Music by Ned Rorem: "Lie With Me, Sweet John."

From *The Grass Harp*, a musical play.
Book and lyrics by Kenward Elmslie, based on the novel by Truman Capote.
Music by Claibe Richardson: "Marry With Me."

From *City Junket*, a musical play *(unfinished)*.
Book and lyrics by Kenward Elmslie, based on his play *City Junket*.
Music by William Elliott: "Who'll Prop Me Up in the Rain."

From *Three Sisters*, an opera.
Libretto by Kenward Elmslie, based on the play by Anton Chekhov.
Music by Thomas Pasatieri: "Andrei's Lament."

From *Lola*, a musical play.
Book and lyrics by Kenward Elmslie.
Music by Claibe Richardson: "Beauty Secrets."

SONG LYRICS II

From *Palais Bimbo Lounge Show*, a revue.
Words by Kenward Elmslie.
Music by Steven Taylor: "Schlock 'n' Sleaze R&B."

From *Postcards on Parade*, a musical play.
Book & lyrics by Kenward Elmslie.
Music by Steven Taylor: "Seventeen Years of Living Hell," "Moments in Time," and "It's a Good Life."
Music by Kenward Elmslie: "Take Me Away, Roy Rogers."

From *Night Emerald*, a musical play (inspired by the life of Oscar Wilde).
Book & lyrics by Kenward Elmslie.
Music by Steven Taylor: "Lads," "Somdomite," "A Secret Sacred Niche," "Love Song," and "Envoi."

In SONG LYRICS II, "Schlock 'n' Sleaze R&B" was based on *Bimbo Dirt* by Kenward Elmslie. Drawings by Ken Tisa.

The poems in *Sung Sex* appeared opposite drawings by Joe Brainard.

POEMS 1991–1998

"Champ Dust" was first published by *The New Censorship* March, 1994 with eight drawings by Joe Brainard that originally appeared in the Black Sparrow edition of *The Champ*. "Local Branch" appeared in *o-blek #10* (1991). "Animals in the Walls" was published in a broadside, *Writing for Bernadette* (1995). "Forty Sonnet" appeared in *The World #45* (1992). The following poems were first published in 1997: "Jakarta Night Arrival," "Welcome Home," and "Fiscal Nonsense" appeared in *New American Writing #15*. *Santa Monica Review* published "Sunday in Dunedin," and "Happy Re-return" appeared in *Bathos Journal*. In 1998, *New American Writing #16* published "Panopticon for Calamity Winifred" and "Outback Taunt."